SIRENS IN THE NIGHT

A CHARLIE MACCREADY MYSTERY

SIRENS IN THE NIGHT

A CHARLIE MACCREADY MYSTERY

James M. McCracken

Copyright © 2020 James M. McCracken

JK Press

2nd Edition

ISBN-13: 978-1-7359233-3-8

All rights reserved. No part of this book may be reproduced or transmitted in any form or by any means, electronic or mechanical, including photocopying, recording, or by any information storage and retrieval system, without permission in writing from the copyright owner.

This is a work of fiction. Names, characters, places and incidents are either the product of the author's imagination or are used fictitiously, and any resemblance to any actual persons, living or dead, events, or locales is entirely coincidental.

CONTENTS

1. THE NEW KID — 1
2. GUS — 10
3. BLACK BUTTE — 22
4. FATHER CECIL — 28
5. CANDLE MAKING — 43
6. THE BURNING BUSH — 60
7. THE DEATH KNELL — 67
8. THE MAP — 86
9. SMOKE — 94
10. FIRE — 106
11. SIRENS IN THE NIGHT — 115
12. A PYROMANIAC IN OUR MIDST — 125
13. A HISTORY LESSON — 136
14. THE QUESTIONING — 142
15. HALLOWEEN — 152
16. THE POLYGRAPH TEST — 163
17. CHRISTMAS — 172
18. ACCUSATIONS — 191
19. DEVRIES — 198
20. THE TOWER — 205
21. THE MUSEUM — 212
22. THE RUINS — 219

DEDICATION

In memory of my nephew,
Terrence Alcott Wilson, II,
"Ted Wilson."
He was so thrilled to point out that,
unbeknownst to me,
I put him in my story.
I only wish he could have read the
entire series.

ACKNOWLEDGMENTS

With sincere appreciation to Dennis Blakesley, Melissa Ainsworth, Mariam Cowgill, Sunny Barber, Helen Granada, James Cowan and Pam Bainbridge-Cowan for their continued encouragement and support.

THE NEW KID

The air smelled fresh, the way it does after a good rain. It was a mixture of the scent of newly mown lawn and the sweet perfume of lilacs in full bloom. The odor tickled Charlie MacCready's nose. He let out a sneeze that echoed off the trees surrounding the Great Lawn of Saint Michael's Abbey and Home for Boys.

"Gesundheit," Howard said.

Charlie smiled at his best friend and wiped his hand on his uniform.

"Hey, look at that," Rick said.

Charlie glanced at Rick and Dale before looking to where Rick was pointing.

A young boy stepped out of the Abbey's black van and looked around. His dark brown hair was short and reminded Charlie of the haircuts the soldiers had in the old army pictures in his history book. The boy looked too well-groomed in his navy-blue suit and a white shirt with a blue tie. He stood beside the van, looking around as though waiting for something or someone.

Father Vicar, the tall thin monk who looked more sinister than holy, walked around the front of the van and started toward the Abbey. His back was rigidly straight, his arms folded over his chest beneath his robes. He moved so smoothly that he appeared to be gliding above the front lawn.

The boy jumped, and quickly retrieved his matching suitcases from the back of the van. Closing the doors, he hurried after the stone-faced monk.

Charlie watched the boy struggle with his suitcases, lagging farther and farther behind. He could not help but remember the day when he arrived at Saint Michael's Abbey & Home for Boys. It was nearly two years since he made that same walk. Nearly two years since his mother's older brother, his Uncle Chester, sent him away from his grandmother's home on Tam O'Shanter Drive to live in the orphanage.

But he's wrong! Charlie thought to himself. I am not an orphan! My parents are alive and one day they will come for me. They have to, they promised.

That was twelve years ago. Charlie was only two when they dropped him off at his grandmother's house in the middle of the night. His mother promised they would return for him. It was that promise Charlie clung to just as tightly as he gripped the old, tarnished, brass key that hung from a gold chain around his neck. His grandmother, Ophelia, had given it to him on the day he was sent away. She gave it with a warning: "Never let it out of your sight or give it to anyone." However, she would not tell him why or what it opened.

Carefully, Charlie opened the locket that also hung from the chain around his neck. He looked at the tiny photograph inside. The miniature image of his parents, Patrick and Faith MacCready, smiled up at him. He snapped the locket closed and looked at the Saint Christopher medal next to it, another gift and another mystery from his grandmother. He turned it over, squinting to read the etching on its back.

"So, who's the new kid?"

"Wha—?" Charlie asked absentmindedly, and looked at the boy again. "Oh, him." He tucked his treasures safely beneath his robes. The black cassock and colored surplice were the uniform worn by all the boys. The color of the surplice indicated to which of the four dormitories a boy belonged. The boys from Saint Thomas, one of two smaller dormitories, wore yellow. The boys from Saint Sebastian, the other small dormitory, wore blue. Those from Saint Peter wore purple, while the members of Saint Nicholas dorm wore red. The only exceptions to this code were the members of The Altar Boys Club. These boys, selected by the head of the Abbey, Abbot Ambrose, and announced each year on All Saint's Day, wore white surplices with lace trim on the billowing sleeves and bottom hem. Charlie, as well as his best friend Howard Miller, were members of that group, and members of Saint Nicholas dorm.

"Do you know him?" Howard asked, continuing to watch the boy scurry after Father Vicar.

"No," Charlie answered, shaking his head.

"He's sure staring at you," Howard said, and made a face at the boy. "I wonder why Abbot Ambrose didn't tell me about him. He always tells me about any new kids moving in. Like when he told me about you, remember?"

"Yeah," Charlie answered with a nod. He also remembered how Howard unselfishly gave up an opportunity to be adopted because he did not want to leave Charlie behind. It was a gesture of friendship Charlie vowed never to forget.

Cautiously, Rick Walters, another Altar Boy and member of Saint Nicholas dorm, stepped up beside Charlie. "His name is Kenneth J. DeVries," he said, watching the boy.

Howard glared at Rick. "How do you know?"

"I have my sources," he snarled back.

"Yeah, I bet," Howard laughed, and turned to face Rick. "You know, we're still mad at you for stealing Charlie's mail."

"I told you, I didn't *steal* it," Rick protested. "Really, Charlie, honest, I was just holding it for you."

Charlie looked at Rick. The image of the stack of letters from his grandmother hidden in the bottom of Rick's nightstand flashed in his mind. His anger rekindled.

"Shall we see what Father Mark thinks?" Howard asked.

"No!" Rick answered quickly. "Okay! Okay, I admit it, I stole your letters but—"

"Aha!" Howard shouted triumphantly. "He finally admits it."

"I didn't do it to hurt you," Rick said, ignoring Howard. "I did it because I was jealous of your friendship. I never had a friend like the two of you guys."

Charlie rolled his eyes and turned his attention back to the new boy. "So, do you know anything more about this Kenneth person?"

"Fa—I mean, my source says Kenneth is a year older than us. His parents died and he was living with his uncle. They were wealthy and left him a fortune."

"So, what's he doing here?" Howard asked.

"I guess he is thinking of becoming a priest."

"Well, if you ask me, he's a bit too prissy looking."

"Howard!" Charlie gasped.

"What? Look at him. He obviously cares too much about the way he looks." Howard looked back at Kenneth.

Kenneth was still staring at them as he followed Father Vicar. His eyes were locked on Charlie's.

"Watch out!" Charlie screamed.

Kenneth tripped over a rock at the edge of one of the many ponds that dotted the Great Lawn. His suitcases flew into the air and he fell face first into the cold water, his luggage splashing down on either side of him.

"Master DeVries!" Father Vicar shouted sternly. "Stop dawdling and hurry up!"

Amid the sounds of Howard's laughter, Kenneth quickly stood up and grabbed his suitcases. He glared at Charlie and Howard before hurrying after Father Vicar.

"You should be careful," Rick warned. "I also heard he's going to be in our dorm now that Gus is leaving."

The smile immediately faded from Howard's face. He looked at the Abbey in the distance. Charlie understood.

"M-m-maybe we sh-sh-should head back to the Abbey. It's almost time f-f-for dinner," Dale suggested.

"Good idea," Charlie agreed. "Come on, Howard." He put his arm around Howard's shoulders.

"I am getting hungry," Howard admitted with a nod, and set out for the Abbey.

Charlie looked at their fellow classmate Dale Kaufman, a member of Saint Sebastian dorm. He was about the same height and weight as Charlie, with dark hair and freckles. "You coming?"

"Y-y-yes," Dale stammered with a frustrated nod. Charlie knew Dale hated that he stuttered. "It's a heredity thing," Dale had explained. "Aggravated by tragically losing one's parents, my shrink claims." Hours of counseling and speech therapy classes had done little to correct it, and Dale had given up on both. He and Rick followed after Howard and Charlie.

As they neared the Abbey building, their thoughts turned to their friend, Gustav Kugele. Gus, a shy, pudgy boy with straight, sandy-blonde hair and a German accent, had come to the Abbey's Home for Boys five years ago after the sudden death of his parents. Howard had taken a liking to him, though it was a bittersweet friendship. At times, Howard seemed overly critical of Gus, quickly becoming annoyed; but at other times, they acted like the best of friends. Howard was shocked, yet proud, when Gus stood up to the bullies in Saint Peter dorm and gave them what for at the start of the last school year.

However, news that Gus's distant cousins from Germany were adopting him and that he was moving away, had hit Howard hard. Though Charlie knew Howard would never admit it, Howard was going to miss his chubby friend just as much as the rest of them.

The sun's rays began to feel warm against the black of Charlie's cassock. He tugged at the collar in an attempt to allow some air beneath his robes and relieve the heat that was building up. He was not about to complain, though. The sun was an all-too-welcome change after weeks of being stuck indoors, cramming for final exams. He took a deep breath, and hurried across the Great Lawn closely behind Howard.

The four boys made their way around the small ponds surrounded by colorful flowerbeds and shade trees that dotted the Great Lawn in front of the Abbey building. The four-story brick building, with its large portico over the main doors, arches, pillars and tiled roof, stood at the south end of the hilltop. From the air, the Abbey building looked like a giant E with its arms stretching southward. "A perfect example of Roman architecture," Prior Emmanuel's words echoed in Charlie's ears.

"I'm really gonna miss Gus," Charlie said out loud, silencing the rambling thoughts in his head.

"M-m-me too," Dale agreed.

"I wish I felt better about this whole thing. I mean, I just have a bad feeling something's not right," Charlie continued.

"What do you mean?" Rick spoke up. "You don't think they're really his cousins?"

Howard stopped and turned around sharply.

"What do you mean by that?" he demanded, glaring at Rick.

"Nothing," Rick answered quickly. Though he was just as tall and just as thin as Howard, he cowered and kept a safe distance away. "I just find it odd that Abbot Ambrose couldn't find them, and yet Father Mark gets appointed as Dean, is here only two months, and poof! Cousins suddenly appear. That's all."

Howard looked at Charlie. He recognized the look in Charlie's brown eyes. "They *are* his cousins, Charlie," he said firmly. "They were in Germany all this time and didn't know what happened to Gus's parents. That's all. No big mystery here." Howard turned back to Rick and scowled. "Just knock it off."

Rick turned his head to avoid Howard's heated breath. "Whatever you say."

"Charlie, don't listen to him," Howard said, turning his back on Rick and looking at his best friend. "He doesn't know anything. You know Abbot Ambrose wouldn't let just anyone adopt Gus."

Charlie thought for a moment. He knew Howard was right, but Rick's comments had only added fuel to the doubts he already had about Gus's cousins.

Frustrated, Howard ran his long, bony fingers through his short, curly, black hair, then pushed his glasses back up on his nose.

"You sh-sh-should get those f-f-fixed," Dale stammered looking at the masking tape that held the bridge of Howard's thick, black-rimmed glasses together.

"Father Mark's trying to see what he can do about getting me a new pair," Howard answered. He let out a heavy sigh as his thoughts returned to his absent friend. "I don't mean to sound selfish, but I wish Gus were staying. I don't want him to go."

"I know," said Charlie, nodding in agreement.

As the four boys neared the Abbey, they stopped dead in their tracks. There, sitting on the front steps beneath the portico, was Gus with his tattered suitcase and a cardboard box. His short, sandy-blonde hair was still damp from his quick shower. His shirt looked freshly pressed and his slacks were nicely creased. Gus glanced at his wristwatch, then at the driveway, seemingly on purpose ignoring his four friends.

"I thought his cousins were supposed to be here already?" Charlie whispered to Howard.

"Let's find out," Howard said. He marched across the circular driveway heading straight for Gus. "Hey, Gus," he greeted him, as though nothing had changed.

"Hi," Gus answered, keeping his eyes on the driveway.

"So, your cousins aren't here yet?" Howard said more than asked.

"Nope." Gus shook his head. "But they *will* be here soon!"

"Good," Howard answered with a nod. "Well, see ya' round." He quickly rushed up the front steps.

"Take care, Gus and don't forget to write." Charlie forced a smile and patted him on the back, then followed Howard.

Dale just nodded and smiled at Gus as he joined Howard and Charlie at the top of the steps.

"Come on, Rick!" Howard ordered when he saw Rick hesitate.

Obediently, Rick rushed up the steps.

They entered the main lobby of the Abbey. Its white marble floor sparkled in the light of the polished brass chandelier hanging above their heads. Directly in front of them were the large, ornately carved, oak doors, the main doors to the Abbey's Church. To their right, a set of plain, oak, double doors led to the monastery wing. To their left, another set leading to the student wing. The bell rang out, signaling it was time for dinner, just as the four entered the Students Wing.

GUS

Outside the refectory on the first floor of the student wing, the boys silently made four lines according to their dormitories. Charlie took his place behind Howard. He glanced at the boys of Saint Peter dorm, and noticed the new boy from the Great Lawn dressed in their robes. He appeared to be upset with Ted Wilson, who stood in line behind him. Dougary Duggan, the notorious troublemaker and ringleader of a small band of thugs who was named into the Altar Boys Club at the last announcement ceremony, was turned around talking to Kenneth. Charlie frowned as he imagined how Dougary was poisoning the new boy's mind against everyone, especially the boys from Saint Nicholas dorm. He nudged Howard and nodded for him to look.

"I thought Rick said he was going to be in our dorm?" he whispered.

Howard shook his head. "He doesn't know anything."

The refectory doors opened and, one row at a time, the boys entered. Silently, they passed in front of the head table on the raised platform at the front of the refectory. The four dorm prefects and the dean stood behind their chairs and inspected the boys as each took his place at one of the four long, wooden tables that stretched out before them.

Charlie looked at the empty place across the table from him where Gus usually sat. He took a slow, deep breath and looked away.

All four walls of the refectory were a cold, sterile, off-white. On the west wall, beginning just a foot away from the double doors and extending to the back of the hall, hung large portraits of the Abbey's "Abbots-Gone-By", as the boys called them, in ornate, gold frames. Behind the head table, on the south wall, hung royal blue, velvet curtains, the only real color in the room. Behind Charlie, on the east wall, tall windows overlooked the forest outside.

Charlie looked at the head table. Brother Conrad, the tall prefect of Saint Thomas the Doubter dorm, stood at his place at the end of the table nearest the doors and smiled warmly at his boys. Beside him stood Father Vicar, the prefect of Saint Peter. He never smiled, except for the wrong reasons. It was well known among the boys that Father Vicar was not pleased that he was passed over for the job of dean last fall.

Father Mark, the Dean, the "prefect of the prefects," as he explained his job, stood beside Father Vicar. However, he was more than just the Dean. For the resident boys, orphaned boys, he was their new father figure. He was not as tall as Father Vicar, maybe two inches shorter; but then again, Father Vicar always did stretch his neck to appear bigger than life. Father Mark was a sturdy man, with blonde hair and blue eyes. Though he and Charlie had a rather shaky start, they made amends and were now friends.

However, they would never have the close relationship like Charlie shared with Abbot Ambrose. Abbot Ambrose, the head of the monastery and Father Mark's superior, stood to the right of Father Mark. His hair was completely white, as was his short beard. He wore a pair of gold-framed, half-moon spectacles on the end of his narrow nose. His gray-blue eyes sparkled as he looked out at his charges. Charlie smiled as he looked at his great-uncle, a secret they shared only with themselves.

Next to Abbot Ambrose stood the first monk Charlie had ever met, Brother Simon, the prefect of Saint Nicholas dormitory. At first Charlie, like the rest of the boys, had the impression that Brother Simon was a twin of Father Vicar with a heart as black as his robes. But that image was changed, at least for Charlie. He knew a different side of Brother Simon. One that Brother Simon kept hidden from the other boys, his warm, caring side.

The last monk, standing beside Brother Simon, was Brother Owen, the prefect of Saint Sebastian dorm. He was a quiet monk and very protective of his boys, of whom Dale was one. For a moment Brother Owen's gaze met Charlie's and his eyes narrowed in a disdainful glare. Charlie looked away, realizing that Brother Owen still did not believe that he had nothing to do with Dale getting hurt the previous autumn.

After the prayer and the clap of the small wooden block against the head table, the signal that it was okay for the boys to talk, the familiar din rose all around them. Charlie looked across the table at Gus's empty chair, then at Rick seated beside it.

"So, what are your plans for this summer?" Rick spoke up with his usual haughty tone.

Charlie ignored him and looked back at his plate.

"All I want to know is," Howard said dryly as he slowly looked up from his plate of roast beef and red potatoes. "When are you going home?"

Rick glared at Howard. "I'm going home tonight after

dinner." He turned back to Charlie. "I don't know what we're going to do this summer. Maybe a cruise or trip to New Orleans or Mexico or—"

"I'm sorry," Charlie cut him off, looking around the room, "Do I look like someone who cares?"

"Very funny," Rick retorted. "Well excuse me for trying to lighten the mood at this table. Gus would be so flattered to know his dorm has gone into mourning over his leaving. Well, I'm not. I'm going to enjoy my summer."

"You do that, Rick," Howard spoke up. "And while you're at it, keep it to yourself!"

"Your jealousy is touching, Howie. Have fun in your pottery class. It sounds like so much fun."

"Who said we're taking pottery this summer?" Howard growled. "Just shut up and eat your dinner."

Charlie could tell that Howard, like himself for that matter, was not in the mood to talk, much less listen to Rick's ramblings.

"My, my," Rick continued. "You better be careful, Howie. Someone might think you actually liked Gus."

"Well, I do and I don't care who knows," Howard snapped back. "He was my friend, unlike you. And stop calling me Howie unless you'd like a punch in that beak you call a nose."

Rick's mouth dropped open. He sat and stared in shock at Howard's reaction. "Well!" he said in a huff. "You're one to talk. Have you looked in a mirror yourself?"

"Oh, will you two just knock it off!" Charlie snapped. "I have a question for you, Rick. I thought you said your 'source' told you the new kid was going to be in our dorm."

"Yes, that's what he said," Rick answered.

"Then why is he sitting at Saint Peter table?"

Rick turned around and looked behind him at Kenneth and

the other boys of Saint Peter. Slowly he turned back around with a puzzled expression. "That's odd."

"You're odd!" Howard sneered.

Rick glared at Howard for a moment and returned to eating his dinner in silence. Howard did the same.

At the end of the meal, after the usual end of the school year announcements, Father Mark paused and smiled.

"I would like you all to welcome the newest member of our family," he said, and stretched out his hand toward Saint Peter table. "Master Kenneth J. DeVries, the Third."

Kenneth slowly rose to his feet as the refectory erupted in a round of applause. He ducked his head slightly, smiled, and nodded piously. His dark brown eyes quickly scanned the assembly as though sizing everyone up, Charlie thought. Once the applause quieted down, Kenneth took his seat again. Dougary slapped him on the back and whispered something into his ear. Charlie knew it was not good.

"Just one more announcement," Father Mark said. He turned toward the boys seated at Saint Nicholas table. "Masters Miller, MacCready and," he glanced over at Saint Sebastian table, "Kaufman, Abbot Ambrose and I would like a word with you after the meal."

"O-o-o," Rick taunted, leaning across the table. "What have you three done now?"

"Nothing!" Howard snapped.

"Just shut up, Rick!" Charlie barked quietly. He flashed a concerned look at Howard. "What do you think they want?" he whispered.

"I don't know." Howard shrugged. "Guess we'll find out soon enough."

The boys rose to their feet, and after the closing prayer, they were dismissed.

"Well, I'd love to stick around and hear what trouble you guys are in, but my parents will be here soon," Rick ribbed.

"Don't let us keep you," Howard brushed him off.

"Yeah, you have a good summer and see you in the fall," Charlie added in mocked sincerity. "Come on," he said to Howard. "Let's get Dale and see what Abbot Ambrose wants."

The two walked off, leaving Rick behind.

In the hallway, Dale was waiting with Father Mark and Abbot Ambrose.

"Come to my office, please," Abbot Ambrose instructed. He tucked his hands beneath his robes and headed down the hall toward his office by the main doors of the student wing. The boys and Father Mark followed. No one said a word. Only the sounds of the soles of their shoes against the marble floor disturbed the silence. Charlie glanced to his right and left as they passed the closed doors of the visitation rooms.

Abbot Ambrose opened his office door and invited them inside. The wall, opposite the door, was lined with oak bookcases filled with books that Charlie was sure his great-uncle had read. Plants and a few framed photographs, set on top of the file cabinet, coffee table and large oak desk added a personal touch to the room. Abbot Ambrose directed the boys to sit in the three chairs to the right of his desk. He sat in his chair behind his desk. Father Mark closed the door and leaned against it.

"The reason we have asked you here," Abbot Ambrose began, "is that we have a favor to ask of you."

"Sure," Howard spoke up eagerly, sitting forward.

Abbot Ambrose put up a halting hand. "Master Miller, please."

Howard sat back in his chair and was silent.

"We know that you boys are close friends with Master

Kugele," he continued. "That is why we have asked to speak to you. As you know, Master Kugele's cousins have been spending a lot of time with him and hoped to adopt him."

Hoped? The word echoed in Charlie's ears.

"Unfortunately, at the last minute, they decided they weren't ready for the additional responsibility."

"I knew it!" snapped Howard. "I didn't trust them from day one."

Father Mark cocked his head and looked at Howard, seemingly surprised by his revelation. He glanced at Abbot Ambrose.

"That is all well and good, Master Miller," Abbot Ambrose said graciously. "However, Master Kugele did not find out until just before supper. Understandably, he is very upset by the news. I would ask the three of you to stay close to him this summer and help him get through this great disappointment. Can you do that?"

"Of course, we can," Charlie answered for the three.

"I knew we could count on you," Abbot Ambrose smiled and nodded.

"Where's G-G-Gus now?" Dale asked.

"I believe he is in the bell tower." Abbot Ambrose smiled at Howard.

Howard looked at Father Mark in open-mouthed shock. He knew Abbot Ambrose had known about his secret place, but Father Mark?

Father Mark smiled and gave Howard a reassuring wink.

"I'm sure Master Kugele would like to see you boys right away," Abbot Ambrose urged.

"Yes," Howard nodded.

"Thank you for letting us know," Charlie said as the three stood up.

"You are welcome."

Once back in the hall, the boys headed for the stairs.

"I can't believe this has happened again!" Howard cursed, shaking his head in disbelief.

"Again?" Charlie asked in surprise. "What do you mean, again? This happened before?"

"Yes. About a year after Gus arrived, a couple showed up here. They took a liking to him and started spending more and more time with him. They bought him candy, toys, clothes and even promised him a new bicycle. They talked about adopting him. Even going as far as asking him how he would like his new bedroom painted and set up. Then one day they just stopped coming. Gus took it hard. For weeks, it was touch and go, but he finally got over it with Prior Emmanuel's and my help. But now...."

"Well, this time he's got the three of us," Charlie said, firmly determined. "We'll get him through this."

"Th-th-that's right," agreed Dale.

"I don't know how much more disappointment he can take," Howard said. "I'm really worried this time."

The boys rushed up the stairs to the fourth floor. As they reached the landing, they turned away from the fire doors and walked over to the small door that led to the bell tower. Without hesitation, Howard opened the door and climbed inside. Charlie and Dale quickly followed him, closing the door behind them.

Even though he had been in the bell tower many times over the last school year, Charlie was still uneasy. Feeling the wooden floor shake beneath his feet, he pressed his back against the brick wall. The hard globs of mortar dug into his back. Slowly his eyes adjusted to the darkness. In the dim light from a hole in the center of the ceiling Charlie could see the three ropes that were attached to the bells in the belfry and dropped through a square opening in the middle of the floor in front of him. He looked to his right at the rickety wooden staircase and saw Howard and Dale already ascending it toward another opening in the ceiling.

"You coming?" Howard asked looking over his shoulder.

"Right behind you," Charlie answered. He took a deep breath and inched his way over to the stairs.

"At least he remembered not to close the trap door," Howard said as he reached the top.

"Wha-wha-why is th-th-that important?" Dale asked.

"You have to leave it open because there is no way to open it from the top if it gets closed," Howard explained.

"Oh," Dale said. He stepped into the belfry. "Wow!" he breathed looking at the views through the four arched, glassless window openings, ignoring the massive bells that hung in the center of the tower.

Charlie entered the belfry and spotted Gus immediately. Suddenly his knees felt weak. Gus sat perched in the south arch, his legs and feet dangling high above the ground below. Nothing prevented him from falling except his balance, and knowing how clumsy Gus was, frightened Charlie even more.

Howard had spotted Gus too. He slowly inched closer, not taking his eyes off his friend.

"Gus?" he said quietly, so as not to scare him.

Gus slowly turned his head and looked at Howard, Charlie and Dale. It was obvious he had been crying. He wiped his nose on the back of his hand.

"'pose you heard," Gus said, looking away.

"Yeah." Charlie said. "Come on down from there, please."

"Sure." Gus nodded. He shifted his weight and swung one of his legs over the sill and into the tower. Suddenly, he began to teeter as he lost his balance.

Charlie gasped and lunged for him.

Howard did the same and was first to grab hold of Gus's arm. With a sharp tug, he pulled Gus off the sill, the two falling on the floor with Gus on top of Howard.

"Ugh!" Howard groaned under Gus's weight. "Get off me." He pushed at Gus.

Gus scrambled to his feet.

"You okay?" Charlie asked.

"Just a few broken ribs," Howard teased, and groaned as he stood up.

"Not you," Charlie said, "Gus."

"Well, thanks a lot," Howard said in mock offense.

"I'm okay," Gus said, sounding less than truthful.

"We're all so sorry," Howard added. "But, look on the bright side, you still have us."

Gus gave them all a blank stare.

"We'll be your family," Charlie said, forcing a smile.

Gus nodded, though it was obvious he was still disappointed.

"Say, you in the mood for a big banana split?" Howard tried to tempt him. "Let's go down to the kitchen and see if we can con Sister Anthony out of a few scoops of ice cream and bananas."

"Don't forget the toppings and whipped cream," Charlie added.

Not giving Gus a choice, Howard put his arm around Gus's shoulders and led him over to the trap door. The four made their way back down to the fourth floor, then down to the kitchen on the first floor.

Sister Anthony, tall and almost manly in her appearance, was busy washing the last of the huge pots used to cook that night's dinner. She glanced over her shoulder at the four as they walked into the kitchen.

"Hi, boys," she smiled. "What may I do for you?"

"Gus, here, has just got some bad news," Howard explained as he cozied up next to her, picking up a dry dishtowel and beginning to dry the wet pots stacked on the drain board. "We were thinking that maybe a few banana splits would cheer him up."

Sister Anthony dried her hands on her apron and looked at Gus. "I'm sorry to hear about your cousins," she sympathized. "Let's see what we can find for you boys." She started for the large, walk-in freezer across the room but paused when she noticed Howard had set the dishtowel down. "Oh, Master Miller, don't stop now. You have five more pots to dry," she said with a smile, pointing at the other pots dripping on the counter.

"But—"

"It was your idea," she said with a shrug and a smile. "Master Kaufman, the banana split bowls are in the cupboard behind you. Master MacCready, the toppings are in the pantry," she instructed and pointed them in the right direction.

The boys quickly retrieved all of the utensils and fixings and gathered around the butcher-block table in the center of the kitchen. Sister Anthony returned from the freezer with a five-gallon drum of vanilla ice cream and set it down.

"When you boys are finished," she said. "Please put everything away and wash up."

"We will," Charlie promised.

"Thank you, Master Miller," Sister Anthony said, and took the damp dishtowel from him. She hung it on the drying rail beside the back door. "My ride is here, so I have to go. Have a good night, and may God bless."

"Thank you, again, Sister," Howard called as the back door

closed behind her.

"Wow!" Dale smiled as he scooped up three huge balls of ice cream.

Gus pulled a stool out from beneath the table and sat down. He watched Charlie spoon strawberries, pineapple and chocolate syrup onto the ice cream. Howard added the whipped cream and chopped peanuts then slid the bowl across the table, in front of him. Gus just sat and stared at the melting dessert.

Charlie looked at him while he prepared another dish.

"Aren't you gonna eat it?"

Gus slid the bowl away. "Thanks, you guys, but ice cream isn't gonna work this time." He stood up and headed for the door.

"Gus, wait!" Howard called but Gus kept walking. He set the can of whipped cream down on the table and plopped down on his stool.

Charlie looked at the melting ice cream in front of him. He no longer felt like eating. "Guess we better put all of this away and clean up." He glanced at the doorway again and frowned.

BLACK BUTTE

The sky was a beautiful shade of bright blue, not a cloud in sight. Charlie wiped the sweat from his brow with his shirt sleeve while he looked out from the south window in the top of the bell tower.

"I'm sorry you didn't get into the photography class," he said turning to look at Howard who was staring out of the east window.

"Yeah, maybe I should just give up on it. This is the third summer in a row that I've missed out."

"Well, I for one am happy 'cause we'll be together again, you, me and Gus. Candle making won't be so bad. You'll see."

"Yeah," Howard agreed half-heartedly. "We'll talk after you have sat through a class with Father Blaise."

Charlie gave Howard a curious look. "He can't be as bad as Father Ichabod was last summer in pottery class."

"You'll see," Howard answered, looking down at the forest below.

Charlie shrugged and retuned to staring at the mound in the distance. Absentmindedly, he fumbled with the key and Saint

Christopher medal on the chain around his neck.

"Have you ever gone out there?" he asked, nodding his head in the direction of the butte.

"Where?" Howard asked, turning around and looking out Charlie's window. "Black Butte?"

"Yes." Charlie nodded. "I know you told Gus and me that it was off-limits, but have you ever sneaked out there?"

Howard did not answer. He fidgeted and looked around the tower, trying to avoid eye contact with Charlie.

"Aha!" Charlie laughed excitedly. "You have! You've gone out there!"

"Well, maybe once or twice," Howard whispered. "But even I would be in so much trouble if Abbot Ambrose found out."

"Why? What's out there?"

Howard shrugged. "I don't know. All I saw were the remains of an old stone building overgrown with blackberries. Nothing too exciting."

Charlie thought for a moment as he looked at the floor, then back at the butte. "Remember Prior Anselm? Before he died, he once told me that the second Abbey building was burned down. Do you think that could be it?"

Howard nodded. "It's possible." He looked at the medal Charlie was still fumbling between his fingers. "You ever figure out what's written on the back of that thing?"

Charlie looked at the Saint Christopher medal, a Christmas gift from his grandmother two Christmases ago. He turned it over and strained to make out the etching on its back.

"Not really," Charlie answered. "I think it's an address, though." He held it closer to his eyes. "1896 NW 10 st— I can't make out the rest. It looks like it's worn off."

"Strange," Howard said. "I wonder why someone would

put their address on the back of a medal."

"Maybe if it got lost, the finder would know where to return it?"

"But where's the city and state?" Howard asked, squinting and trying to read the etching.

"There isn't any. It doesn't look like there ever was, either."

"And I suppose your grandmother won't tell you about this either?" Howard asked, but already knew the answer.

"No," Charlie shook his head.

"Well, we'll figure it out soon enough," Howard said and returned to the view from the east window. "Hey look, there's Gus!" He pointed toward the path leading to the cemetery, past the Grotto with its life-sized statue of Mary. The statue was nicknamed Our Lady of the Subway by Novice Stephen years ago because it stood in front of a tunnel which led underground to the garage on the north side of the Great Lawn.

"Where's he going?" Charlie asked, watching Gus slip behind the statue and into the tunnel.

"Beats me."

"Have you talked to him since last night?"

"No." Howard sighed and shook his head. "He was up before me and skipped breakfast this morning."

"Won't he get into trouble with Father Mark?"

"Nah, he's cutting him some slack right now," Howard shrugged. "He's sure taking it harder than I thought. Guess it's harder the second time; not to mention this time it was family and they rejected him."

"Do you think he feels guilty for what he said to you? You know, about your father putting you here and not wanting you?" Charlie asked.

"Nah." Howard shook his head. "We got past that."

Charlie was not convinced. When he looked at Howard's eyes, it was obvious the memory of that day in the tower still bothered him. In the heat of anger, Gus had reminded Howard that his own dad had chosen the wishes of his new wife over him, and put him in the orphanage seven and a half years ago. What was worse, he even gave his permission for Howard to be adopted. At least that was what Howard always said.

"Maybe if we tried to talk to him again?" Charlie suggested.

"I don't know. I sure wish Prior Emmanuel were here. He'd know what to do."

Charlie looked back at the statue of Mary and the tunnel. "Howard, what did you mean that it was 'touch-and-go' with Gus when this happened the first time."

A pained look came over Howard's face.

"What? What happened?" Charlie asked.

Howard leaned against the tower wall beside the window opening. "Gus became destructive."

"Destructive?" Charlie repeated, feeling an uneasiness building inside him. "What do you mean?"

"He began to vandalize things. First it was just writing in his school books, but then he started to damage Abbey property."

"Anything serious?"

"Not really. He just scratched up the finish on his school desk," Howard assured him. "Prior Emmanuel was finally able to get through to him and helped him work it out."

"Maybe we should talk to Prior Emmanuel when he gets back from his retreat with the new postulants?" Charlie suggested.

"I don't know. He's been really busy. I'm not sure if he will have time."

"Do you think Gus will do it again? Be destructive, I mean?"

"I don't know. I don't think so," Howard answered and pushed away from the wall.

Charlie walked back to the south window and looked back at the butte. "Do you suppose we could sneak out there sometime?" he asked, changing the subject.

"Where? Black Butte?" Howard asked, shaking his head. "No! Out of the question!" He walked away from the windows.

"But why? You've been out there," Charlie pleaded, and followed him. "I want to see it too."

"No, and that's final. We best get out of here before the Angelus rings. It's almost noon."

Howard quickly descended the wooden staircase before Charlie could protest further. Charlie carefully followed, closing the trap door behind them.

As they reached the fourth floor and entered the hallway, they noticed a group of boys huddled around Father Vicar and Father Mark. Father Mark was carefully examining a purple surplice, holding it up and smelling it. Charlie tried not to appear interested as he and Howard neared the group, but he strained his ear to listen.

"Suppose you take it from the top," Father Mark said, still looking at the surplice. "When did you notice it was missing?"

Ted Wilson let out an exasperated sigh. "I already told you, last night it was in my locker. This morning, when I was getting ready for breakfast, it was gone."

"Did you leave your locker open and unattended?" Father Mark asked.

"No!" Ted replied.

Father Mark looked at him and raised an eyebrow.

"Mark," Father Vicar spoke up. "This is getting us

nowhere. It is obvious Master Wilson doesn't know what happened."

Father Mark looked at the faces of the boys huddled around them. "Perhaps we should continue this in my office."

"Now really," Father Vicar protested. "Is that necessary?"

"Yes, Vicar, it is," Father Mark answered, looking him straight in the eyes. "Master Wilson claims he doesn't know how this happened to his surplice, and yet he insists that no one else had access to it. Obviously, he is either forgetting something, he is covering up for someone else, or he did it himself.

"So, Master Wilson, Vicar, my office after lunch. I suggest the rest of you boys not be late for lunch."

"Yes, Father," the boys said and quickly scattered.

Charlie watched as Father Mark folded up the surplice and headed down the stairs.

"What was that all about?" Charlie whispered to Howard.

"Beats me," Howard said, shaking his head. "But I'll find out."

The two continued on their way back to their dorm to change for lunch.

FATHER CECIL

Charlie stared at his reflection in the mirror. He wet his comb again and quickly ran it through his auburn hair. He wanted to make a good first impression on his new assignment. In the meeting of the Altar Boys Club after lunch, Charlie was told he would be assisting Father Cecil. However, today, as with every other day, Charlie's hair was not cooperating. He stared at his reflection, at his damp hair. "Why do I bother?" he muttered to himself. He put his comb down and pressed his ears against the sides of his head with his flattened palms.

"That's not gonna help," Howard said with a slight laugh. "I wish you wouldn't be so self-conscious. Your ears really don't stick out *that* much."

Charlie did not hear a word. His hands were still covering his ears. He quickly grabbed his comb and turned to follow but noticed Gus. Gus was standing at the end of the row of sinks. He looked as though he were about to be sick. His face was pale and tiny beads of sweat dotted his forehead. Cautiously, Charlie moved to the sink beside him.

"Are you nervous about meeting Father Benedict?" Charlie

asked.

Gus just gave him a blank stare as though he did not hear or had not understood what he said.

"Don't worry," Charlie continued. "I hear Father Benedict's a nice guy. You'll like him."

Gus shrugged indifferently.

"Gus, are you okay?"

"Yeah," Gus answered with a slight edge in his voice. "Why shouldn't I be?" He looked around the wash room with its rows of white porcelain sinks, mirrors and cold white tiled walls. "I still have this place to call home. Who needs a stupid family anyway?" He brushed past Charlie, intentionally bumping shoulders aggressively. Charlie turned around and watched Gus disappear down the stairs.

Moments later, as Charlie stood in front of Father Cecil's door, he became aware of the butterflies in his own stomach. He took a deep breath and knocked lightly on the plain oak door. He glanced up at the crucifix that hung to the left of the door and noticed a row of raised dots on a metal strip beneath it. He reached up and touched them just as the door opened.

"Who's there?" asked the middle-aged monk. His milky blue eyes looked straight at Charlie. "Who's there?" he repeated.

"Master MacCready, Charlie MacCready, Father," Charlie answered hesitantly.

"Ah, yes," Father Cecil said as he reached out his hand and grabbed Charlie's shoulder. His hand felt its way toward Charlie's neck.

Instinctively, Charlie pulled away, grabbing the key beneath his robes.

"Don't be afraid, son," Father Cecil said as he stepped back into his room. "Didn't Mark tell you that I'm blind?"

"Blind? No, sir—I mean, no, Father," Charlie corrected himself. "He didn't."

Charlie stepped into the small room. He looked around. The walls were bare, void of any decoration except for a large crucifix that hung above the head of the single bed. The bed sat in the corner against the wall directly inside the door. Beside the head of the bed was a large window. Its curtains had been drawn to allow the daylight in; otherwise there was no other light in the room. In the opposite corner from the bed, on the other side of the window, was a wingback chair and small side table. The remaining furniture was a round, wooden table with two matching chairs, set just to the left of the front door.

"Well, that's Mark for you," Father Cecil said as he walked straight over to his chair in the corner and sat down. "He's always trying to find humor at my expense. Don't move that!"

Charlie jumped and took his hand off the wooden chair. "But? How?"

"I'm blind, not deaf," Father Cecil answered. "It's important that you do not move anything in the room. I know my way around and if anything is moved, I could trip over it. Just sit in the chair that is already pulled out.

"And one other thing," Father Cecil continued. "When answering a question, please use your voice. I can't hear you when you gesture or nod."

"Yes, sir—Father," Charlie answered.

"Please, you don't have to be so formal," Father Cecil said. "So, how old are you, son?"

"I'm fourteen, but soon to be fifteen."

"How long have you been here at Saint Michael's?"

"Nearly two years, but I'm not an orphan. My parents are still alive," Charlie quickly added.

"Oh, I see." Father Cecil nodded knowingly. "So, what did

you do to get sent here?"

"Nothing," Charlie blurted. "I mean, I'm not a juvenile delinquent or anything."

"Oh, forgive me, my mistake," Father Cecil apologized. "So, do you think you have a vocation to the priesthood?"

Charlie started to answer but then stopped and thought. "I don't know," he answered quietly. "Actually, my uncle sent me here because he didn't want me living with my grandmother anymore. Father, may I ask you a question?"

"Have I always been blind?" Father Cecil answered, anticipating Charlie's curiosity.

Charlie nodded then remembered. "Yes," he said.

"No, I haven't always been blind. My sight started going when I was in my mid-twenties. It wasn't until my thirtieth birthday that the lights went out for good. That was five years ago."

"I'm sorry," Charlie said.

"Don't be," Father Cecil said, smiling. "We all have our cross to bear, and this just happens to be mine. A bit of irony: When I entered the monastery sixteen years ago, Abbot Ambrose gave me the name Cecil. The name Cecil means blind." Father Cecil gave a slight laugh.

"I didn't know that," Charlie admitted.

"Don't sound so surprised. All words have a meaning, even names. Do you know what Charlie means?" he asked.

Charlie shook his head and instantly remembered what Father Cecil said. "No," he quickly answered.

"It means, free man. So, now you can impress your friends by telling them what your name means." Father Cecil smiled.

Charlie looked around the room, not knowing what to say. Finally, he looked back at Father Cecil.

"Do you ever leave this room?" he asked, changing the

subject.

Father Cecil smiled and gave a slight laugh. "Yes. I get around. However, as you can imagine, outside of this room it isn't as safe for me. Things get moved around. That's one reason I've asked for the assistance of an Altar Boy. It would be nice to have someone help me who isn't out for a good laugh."

"Well, I would be happy to help you. Did you want to go outside now?"

"No, not now, thank you," Father Cecil said.

Charlie looked around the room again, searching the walls as though he would find something to talk about on its bare surfaces.

"Would you mind reading to me?" Father Cecil asked, breaking the silence.

"No, I wouldn't mind," Charlie answered eagerly.

"Good. Simeon brought me a newspaper this morning; it's on the table there. Could you just tell me the headlines and I will tell you what I would like you to read?"

"Sure." Charlie picked up the newspaper and looked at the date. It was a week old. He hesitated, but then began to read.

The time seemed to fly by as Charlie read article after article aloud to Father Cecil. Before he knew it, it was time for lunch. Charlie guided Father Cecil to the monastery's refectory for his noon meal. He said his goodbyes before hurrying off to join Howard and Gus outside their refectory.

"So, how did it go with Father Cecil?" Howard asked as Charlie took his place in line.

"Pretty good, actually. Did you know he's blind?" Charlie asked.

"No," Howard answered. "I mean, I heard rumors that one of the monks was but I didn't hear who. What did you do?"

"I just read to him all morning. Oh, did you know that his

name, Cecil, means blind?"

"Isn't that tragic," Howard answered, mildly interested.

"What about you?" Charlie asked. "How was Brother Gregory?"

"Same old, same old," Howard answered with a shrug. "Brother Gregory's working on a new project for the new museum. He's making display cases. So I spent the morning sanding pieces of wood. What about you?" Howard turned toward Gus.

"Yeah, what was Father Benedict like?" Charlie cocked his head to see around Howard.

"He's a monk," Gus answered dryly.

"Well, duh, silly," Howard retorted.

Charlie gave Howard a sharp nudge and a glare.

"But, do you like him?" Charlie asked.

"It doesn't matter if I like him or not. He'll be dead in a few years."

"Gus!" Charlie gasped.

"What? It's true."

Howard rolled his eyes and shook his head as he turned around facing Charlie. Charlie recognized the look and dropped the subject, resuming his place in line just as the refectory doors opened. The boys filed inside in silence. After the prayer, they took their seat as the serving brothers began their rounds.

"Hey," Howard said, getting Charlie's and Gus's attention. "Charlie, remember the other day when we saw Father Mark and Father Vicar outside Saint Peter dorm?"

Charlie nodded.

"Well, I found out what was going on."

"You did!" Charlie gasped. "What was it?" he asked, glancing across the table at Gus who was pretending not to listen.

Howard waited until the serving Brother set a plate of lasagna and green salad on the table in front of Gus. He then leaned over the table. "One of the brothers in the laundry discovered that one of Ted Wilson's surplices," Howard paused purposely, looking at their faces. "Was burned."

"Burned?" Charlie repeated, trying to imagine who would have done it. "Do they know how it happened?"

"According to some of the guys who saw it, they said it smelled like cigarette smoke. So maybe he was smoking and somehow did it," Howard answered.

Suddenly Gus's fork slipped from his hand and clanked as it fell against the stoneware plate, landing on the table. He quickly picked it up without looking at either of the boys across from him.

Charlie looked at Gus curiously, then at Howard, remembering their previous conversation. For a split second he wondered if Gus knew more about it than he was letting on. He could tell by the look in Howard's eyes that Howard was thinking the same thing.

Howard sat back in his chair as the serving Brother finished his rounds, setting his lunch before him. He waited quietly, watching as the Brother wheeled his serving cart through the door beside the head table, back into the kitchen. He turned back to Charlie and Gus.

"Ted spent the afternoon in Father Mark's office. He still insists he doesn't know how it happened."

"Does Father Mark believe him?" Charlie asked.

"I guess so," Howard answered, shrugging his shoulders. "Ted's back at the Saint Peter table." He glanced across the refectory at Ted seated next to the new kid, Kenneth.

Charlie looked at Gus who appeared to be indifferent to their conversation as he ate his lunch. Charlie resisted the temptation to ask him if he knew anything about the surplice. Instead, he ate the rest of his lunch in silence.

"So, what are we doing this afternoon?" Charlie asked and took a bite of his ice cream sundae.

"Father Mark is taking me to town to get a new pair of glasses," Howard announced with a smile. He pushed the bridge of his broken glasses up on his nose.

"That's great!" Charlie said. "When are you gonna be back?"

"Don't know. Father Mark said he had some errands to do while in town, so it might be a while."

"That's okay. I'm sure Gus and I can find something to do."

Gus looked up at the sound of his name. "Huh?" he grunted.

"I just said that maybe you and I can hang out this afternoon."

Gus shook his head. "That's okay, I'll pass. I've got my own stuff to do."

"No biggie," Charlie said, sounding a bit disappointed. "I'm sure I can find something to do."

After lunch, Charlie slipped into the bell tower, careful to avoid being seen by the other boys milling about in the hallway outside Saint Peter dorm. After his eyes adjusted to the darkness in the room beneath the bells, he inched his way over to the stairs. Cautiously he climbed the wooden staircase to the top of the tower. The old boards of the staircase seemed to creak louder than usual. Charlie pushed the trap door in the ceiling open. Once in the belfry he walked over to the east window.

The branches of tall fir trees swayed gently in the cool breeze. The leaves of the birch trees shimmered. In the distance, the farmlands looked like a patchwork quilt. Charlie looked up at the cloudless sky and silently wished he could have tagged along with Howard and Father Mark.

Bored, he started to turn away from the window but stopped when he caught sight of Gus. Gus was standing just outside the Grotto of Our Lady of the Subway. He was talking to Kenneth DeVries.

"Oh no, this can't be good," Charlie murmured and shook his head. He squinted, straining his eyes to see what they were doing. Frustrated, he turned around and quickly rushed out of the bell tower. He descended the wooden stairs that shook horribly against the wall.

He climbed out of the small door and back into the fourth-floor stairwell. He paused briefly to beat the dust from his robes then ran down the stairs, careful at each landing so as not to be caught running by any of the monks. Moments later, he emerged from the back door and headed toward the place where he had last seen Gus and Kenneth talking.

To Charlie's relief, Gus was still outside the grotto, his back turned toward the Abbey.

"Hey, Gus," Charlie greeted giving him a friendly slap on the back.

Gus yelled and jumped away. He spun around and quickly shoved his hands into the large pockets of his cassock. "Don't do that!"

"I'm sorry. I didn't mean to startle you." Charlie apologized and looked around. "So, where's the new kid? I was just up in the tower and noticed you were down here talking to him."

"So, what're you doing, spying on me?" Gus tone was defensive and even a bit hostile.

"No. I was just looking around and saw you, that's all. But while we're on the subject, Gus, you shouldn't be hanging out with the likes of him. He's in Saint Peter, remember?"

"Oh, so now you're telling me who I can and can't be friends with?"

"No, I'm just worried about you. I—"

"Why? Because I'm such a loser that not even the only family I have left wants me around and left me in this hellhole?"

"That's not what I was going to say," Charlie tried to defend himself. "I just meant, be careful. You remember the last time you got mixed up with the guys in Saint Peter dorm."

"I don't believe you. Did Howard put you up to this? I thought you were my friends. You won't be happy until I have no family or friends left except you guys. Well, forget it! Kenneth was right about you!" Gus snapped and stormed off in a huff.

"Me?" Charlie said, confused.

Gus did not acknowledge him. He quickly stormed away in a huff.

"Gus!" Charlie called after him, but Gus just ignored him, continuing to walk down the path toward the swimming pool.

Charlie took a step and stopped. He sniffed the air again. There was a faint scent of smoke. He looked around at the ground, searching for the cause of the odor. Then he spotted it. At the edge of the ivy that covered the stone fence and was now encroaching on the path, rose a thin wisp of smoke. Slowly he bent down and picked up a still smoldering cigarette butt.

"Nasty habit," a voice said behind him.

Charlie jumped and spun around.

"Wha—" he said, looking at the smiling nun.

"Smoking is a nasty habit," she repeated, and nodded at the smoldering cigarette in Charlie's hand.

"Oh," he gasped and quickly threw the cigarette butt onto

the ground. "It's not mine, really. I just found it here. Someone must have dropped it." He crushed the smoldering ember out with his shoe.

"I see," the sister said with a suspicious nod. "Well, *someone* should be more careful. *They* wouldn't want to start a fire now, would *they*?"

"No, Sister. I mean, yes, Sister. I mean, no, they wouldn't," Charlie stammered.

"Well, good day to you, Master MacCready." She winked at him before turning and walking away.

A chill ran up Charlie's spine as her parting words echoed in his ears. He watched her walk down the road toward the pig barns, disappearing into the trees. "How did she know my name?" he wondered aloud. He searched his memories but could not recall ever seeing her before. And he was sure he would remember a nun as pretty as her. He glanced down at the smashed cigarette butt and his thoughts returned to Gus. Slowly he headed back to his dormitory.

The minutes seemed to pass like hours. While Charlie waited for Howard to return, he busied himself by writing another letter to his grandmother. She was the only grown up he knew he could trust enough to confide in about Gus. Maybe she would know what to do. When he was finished, he stuffed the letter into the envelope and looked around. The dorm was empty and quiet. He licked the envelope flap and sealed it shut. Just as he affixed the stamp, the dormitory doors opened and Howard walked in.

"Hey, Charlie," he called loudly as he approached their cubicle. "Whadaya think?"

"You got them already?" Charlie said, jumping to his feet.

"So…." Howard fished as he struck a pose, trying to look very studious.

"They're just like your old pair," Charlie answered, laughing at Howard's comical expressions.

Howard turned sharply and looked at Charlie. "No, they aren't."

Charlie recoiled slightly. He took a closer look and thought some more. "Yes, Howard, I'm sorry but I think they are."

Howard let out a laugh. "I know," he admitted. "The eye doc just popped out my old lenses and stuck them in these." He took them off and examined them. "Father Mark convinced him to give them to me for free. He told the doc he didn't have to make a contribution at Mass this Sunday. Father Mark told me in the car he gets a lot of free stuff at the local shops in town. He's even convinced some of the stores to give the seminarians and us a discount on stuff we buy. Isn't that cool?"

"That is," Charlie agreed.

"So, what have you been doing all afternoon?"

"I'm so glad you're back. You won't believe my afternoon."

Just then the bell rang, signaling it was time for dinner. The two boys quickly put their robes on and headed down the hall.

"So, what happened?" Howard asked as they reached the stairwell.

"Well if it isn't the girls from Saint Nichol's ass," Dougary jeered as he, Austin, Larry and Kenneth walked up behind them. Austin intentionally bumped hard into Charlie's shoulder, knocking him off balance and causing him to stumble down two steps and drop his letter. He quickly picked it up and stuffed it into his pocket.

"Watch it, dog breath!" Howard snapped.

"Oh, can't you think of something more original?" Dougary said and yawned. "So, tell us, Chucky, what happened?"

Charlie stopped at the landing and turned to face Dougary and his pals. His eyes met with Kenneth's and he looked back at Dougary. "It's none of your business!" Charlie snapped. "Come on, Howard." He grabbed Howard's arm and the two rushed down the stairs with Dougary and his goons close behind.

"Come on Chucky, you can trust me," Dougary called after them. "We're both Altar Boys, remember?"

Charlie fought the urge to answer, instead he quickened his pace. "We'll talk about it later," he whispered to Howard as they slipped into line outside the refectory. "Meet me in the bell tower after dinner. We'll have some privacy there." He glanced over his shoulder at Dougary, who stood staring at them.

After dinner, Charlie did not waste time changing out of his robes. Instead, he went straight to the bell tower and waited for Howard. He was standing at the south arch, staring out at Black Butte when Howard finally arrived. Howard had changed out of his robes, and was in his blue jeans and white polo shirt emblazoned with the Abbey's crest on the breast pocket.

"Will you just forget about it," he said in disgust. "Honestly, I'm going to quit coming up here with you if you don't."

"I can't help it," Charlie said, turning away from the window. "I just have this feeling there's something out there that I'm supposed to see."

"How many times do I have to tell you, there's nothing out there but a bunch of rocks and some old ruins of a burned-out building."

"See!" Charlie snapped. "You got to see it, so why can't I?"

"You're hopeless. You know that? Hope-less," Howard said, over enunciating the last syllable. He walked over to the east window and looked down. "Hey, look! There's Gus."

"Where?" Charlie asked, walking over to the east window and looking down.

"Right there," Howard answered, pointing in the distance just past Our Lady of the Subway. "But who is that with him?"

"It's Kenneth," Charlie said and turned his back to them.

"You mean, Kenneth J. DeVries, the third," Howard mocked in a nasal tone with his nose in the air.

"The one and only," Charlie added with a frown. "That's what I wanted to talk to you about. This afternoon I came up here and saw them down there. I ran down to see what they were doing but Kenneth was gone."

"So?" Howard said, shrugging his shoulders indifferently.

"When I walked up, Gus acted real nervous, like he was trying to hide something from me. I think he's started smoking," Charlie blurted.

"Smoking?" Howard looked at Charlie. "Are you sure?"

"I think so. I mean after he stormed off, I found a lit cigarette butt."

Howard turned and looked over his shoulder at Gus as Charlie continued.

"If he is, then I think Kenneth may be supplying him with them."

"I'll kill him!" Howard said through clenched teeth.

"Gus?" Charlie asked.

"No," Howard said turning back to face Charlie. "DeVries." He started for the trap door.

"Howard, wait!" Charlie called to him.

Howard stopped and turned back.

"If we go down there, it'll just make matters worse. Gus already thinks we are trying to boss him around, tell him who he can or can't be friends with. He won't listen and will just get madder. Remember the last time he got mixed up with those creeps in Saint Peter, it'll be like that all over again."

Howard thought for a moment. "You're right."

"Maybe we should go to Fa—"

"No!" Howard interrupted.

"But you said, Prior Emmanuel helped Gus the last time."

"He won't be back for another week or more. We can't tell anyone. We have to figure out how to get through to Gus ourselves. If any one of the monks find out and report him, he'll be in so much trouble, I don't even want to imagine."

"But what about Kenneth?"

"But what?"

"Can't we tell Father Mark that Kenneth is giving Gus cigarettes?"

"DeVries will just lie and say Gus stole them. Or even worse, Gus gave them to him," Howard answered. "No, we can't say a word."

Charlie thought for a moment and glanced over his shoulder. Gus and Kenneth were gone. The grotto was empty. He turned back to face Howard.

"Do you think Gus could be the one who burned that surplice?"

Howard looked at Charlie. "Why would you say that?"

"Because you said the last time this happened, Gus was destructive."

Howard did not answer, but turned around and walked over to the trap door. "Come on, let's get out of here."

Charlie quickly followed Howard out of the tower, closing the door behind them.

CANDLE MAKING

The next morning Charlie woke late. No time for a shower before breakfast. He quickly dressed, slipping his white surplice on over his black cassock. He closed his locker door and snapped the lock shut. The dorm was nearly empty. Neither Howard nor Gus were around. Charlie rushed into the hall and headed for the stairs.

Reaching the first floor, he spotted Howard standing in line outside the refectory.

"What happened to you?" Howard asked as Charlie took his place in line.

"Me? Why didn't you wake me?"

"I did, twice," Howard answered.

Charlie looked puzzled. He did not remember Howard waking him. Perhaps he was more tired than he realized. He shrugged it off and looked around.

"Where's Gus?"

"Don't know."

Charlie looked at the Saint Peter line. "Kenneth isn't here either."

Howard glanced in the general direction and shook his head.

"Any thoughts about a plan?" Charlie asked.

"No," Howard answered.

The refectory doors opened and the boys fell silent. They entered the dining hall in their usual single file line. Charlie looked at the head table as he passed in front of it. Father Vicar was whispering something to Father Mark and he appeared angry.

Brother Simon coughed and drew Charlie's attention. He shook his head disapprovingly at Charlie and motioned for him to take his place at his table. Charlie could feel his face turning red, embarrassed that he was caught staring.

After the prayer and the clap from the wooden block, Charlie leaned closer to Howard.

"Did you see that?"

"See what?"

"When we came in Father Vicar was saying something to Father Mark and he didn't look too happy."

"He never does."

"All I could make out was that Father Vicar was saying something about smoke or smoking," Charlie continued, ignoring Howard's disinterested tone.

When Howard did not comment, Charlie turned his attention to his French toast. He sat staring at it. Not really hungry anymore, he looked up just as Gus and Kenneth walked into the refectory. They paused in front of the head table before taking their seat at their respective tables.

"Hi Gus," Charlie greeted.

Gus did not respond. He gave Charlie a quick glance before turning his attention to the plate of food in front of him.

"You want some more?" Charlie offered.

"No, I don't want your scraps," Gus snarled.

Charlie recoiled. "Look, they aren't scraps. I haven't touched them."

Gus rolled his eyes and continued eating his own breakfast. Charlie looked at Howard in shock.

"What?" Howard shrugged. "So, he doesn't want it."

"Well, yeah but—" he agreed yet protested. "But Gus is always hungry."

"Ah, you guys, I'm still here. I can hear you," Gus spoke up sarcastically, syrup dripping down his chin.

"Sorry," Charlie apologized. He began to move his food around on his plate with his fork.

"So, have you heard where our candle making class is going to be?" Howard asked smugly, breaking the long silence.

"No, where?" Charlie asked.

"I heard from one of the upperclassmen that it's going to be in the room next to Father Ichabod's pottery studio," Howard answered.

"That's no big deal," Charlie said, unfazed. "Father Ichabod's okay."

"That's what you say," Howard scoffed, rolling his eyes and shaking his head. "I want to get down there right after we're done so we can beat Dougary and his goons."

"Oh, they're not in our class again, are they?" Charlie groaned.

"'fraid so," Howard answered.

The rest of the meal passed quietly. Charlie could not wait for it to end. The clap from the wooden block silenced what little talking there was in the refectory. Father Mark stood and walked to the front of the head table. He looked at boys and smiled.

"We have a busy day ahead of us," he began. "You should all have your class assignments by now and if you don't, you need to see your dorm prefect immediately after prayer.

"The only other announcement is the Altar Boys will be having a rehearsal for the Novitiate Mass this afternoon. This year is rather exciting for us because one of our novices, familiar to all of you, Novice Stephen, will be making his First Vows."

Charlie smiled. Stephen had been the sacristan, the head Altar Boy and the one in charge of the priest's vestments, during Charlie's first year. Stephen was one of the good guys. Like Howard, he looked out for the others, especially the orphaned boys in his dorm. From one of their long talks that first year, Charlie found out that Stephen's family was killed in a tornado when he was very young. He was taken to an orphanage in the Midwest first, but when it closed, he was sent to St. Michael's. The brothers at the Abbey had become his family.

After the prayer concluded, the boys were dismissed. Gus immediately slipped away through the small crowd exiting the refectory. Charlie started after him but Howard grabbed his arm, stopping him.

"Let him go," he said. "Come on, we'd better get to class. Remember I want to get there before everyone else so we can make sure we all sit together. We can save Gus a seat."

The two headed down the path toward the stone shed. As they passed Our Lady of the Subway, Charlie glanced at the grotto and stopped. He stared curiously at shadow behind the statue.

"Did you see that?" he gasped.

Howard stopped and turned around. "See what?" he asked.

Charlie took a step closer to the ivy hedge separating the grotto from the path. He squinted, trying to see in the dark. Then his shoulders relaxed and he turned back around, facing Howard.

"Oh nothing, I suppose." He shrugged. "I thought I saw

smoke coming from behind the statue."

"Smoke?" Howard repeated, and looked past Charlie. "Are you sure?" The tone in his voice was beginning to alarm Charlie.

"It's nothing. I must have imagined it."

Howard looked at Charlie, then back down the path toward the Abbey. Dougary and his buddies were just coming around the side from the back door.

"Come on, we best be going," he said.

"Okay," Charlie agreed.

As they continued along the path the old stone building came into view. Wild ivy crept up the front, covering two thirds of the façade. Just beyond the large wooden door of the pottery studio was another door to the candle studio. Charlie spotted Father Ichabod, the pottery teacher, standing under a tree smoking his cigarette, while he waited for his new students. He smiled and shook his head remembering how wrong he was about his former teacher; Father Ichabod was the one who saved him from Larry Hertz's father a few weeks before. He was not such a bad guy after all.

"So, are you going to be okay with taking candle making this year?"

"As if I have a choice?" Howard sighed. "What gripes me is that it's the same thing every year. Those jerks in Saint Peter always get to the list first and they take all the good classes."

"But what about Dougary and his goons?" Charlie added. "They seem to purposely wait for us to choose a course so they can sign up for it, too. Why do they insist on tormenting us?"

"Well, let's see," Howard said sarcastically putting a finger to his cheek in mocked deep thought, "your first year you managed to have Dougary's dad committed to the nut house. Then just a few weeks ago you got Larry expelled. Perhaps they just don't like us."

"Ya think?" Charlie laughed.

"We just have to stick together and we'll be okay."

They arrived at the candle studio just as the large, knotted wooden door opened and a tall, thin monk stepped out into the morning light. A smile spread across his crooked lips.

"Morning, boys," Father Blaise greeted in a rather raspy voice and reached out his hand to them.

Charlie tried not to stare as Father Blaise shook Howard's hand. Father Blaise's bald head, face and hands, the only parts of his body that were exposed from beneath his black habit, appeared shiny and unreal, as though he were made of wax. Despite his being tall, Father Blaise's shoulders were beginning to slump with age, though Charlie thought the real reason was that Father Blaise had been in the sun too long and was beginning to melt.

"Good morning, Father," Charlie quickly shook the priest's hand, then wiped his hand on his surplice.

"Now this is what I like to see." Father Blaise smiled. "Boys who take my class seriously and are punctual. Come on in."

Howard opened his mouth as though starting to correct the old monk but Charlie elbowed him in the ribs. Howard coughed and looked at Charlie in surprise.

"Don't say a word," Charlie warned in a hushed whisper. "Let him think we really wanted this class."

"I wasn't going to say anything," Howard fibbed.

Charlie looked around in amazement when he walked into the room. The four walls made of stone and mortar had a waxy sheen to them. The only window in the room, a skylight in the ceiling, appeared covered in a milky film. It was beautiful, yet eerie. An old wooden table sat beneath the skylight in the center of the room. Eight stools were stationed around the table, four on one side and four on the other. A thin book, *Candle Making Made Easy*, was placed on the table in front of each stool. Down the center of the table was a single row of hot plates. In the corner of the room, beneath a dark green chalkboard, sat stacks of wax blocks. On the counter that ran along the opposite wall were several tall, thin pots and various metal candle molds.

Howard quickly took the stool at the end of the table facing the door. Charlie took the stool to Howard's left.

"Dale, grab that stool there," Howard instructed pointing at the stool across from him.

Dale quickly did as he was instructed and continued looking around the room.

"We're going to have a full class this year," Father Blaise said, sounding giddy. "That means we'll have lots and lots of new candles. Oh, this is going to be so much fun." He grinned from ear to ear.

Howard looked at Charlie and rolled his eyes.

Charlie hated to admit it, but Howard might be right about Father Blaise. Although they just met, Charlie was getting the distinct impression that Father Blaise was missing a marble or two.

The door opened and Gus walked into the studio, followed closely by Kenneth, Dougary and Travis.

"Here, Gus," Charlie said, pulling out the stool to his left.

Gus glared at Charlie defiantly and took the seat next to Dale instead.

Dougary quickly grabbed the seat at the end of the table, with Kenneth on his left next to Gus and Travis across from him, leaving one empty stool beside Charlie.

"I see everyone is here. Very good, very good," Father Blaise beamed. "Let's get started, shall we?"

"Let's not and say we did," Dougary sneered under his

breath but loud enough for all to hear.

Father Blaise pretended not to hear, and moved to the end of the table between Gus and Howard. "I see a couple of new faces with us. So why don't we get started by introducing ourselves to each other? Just say your name, what dorm you are in, and whatever else you would like us to know about you."

"I'll begin." He smiled. "My name is Father Blaise. I've been teaching candle making for nearly thirty-six years. It's been a very fulfilling assignment, and, I'm not too humble to admit, a might profitable, too. All of the candles we make are sold at our booth during Oktoberfest and in our gift shops. A little bit of trivia. In a strange coincidence, Saint Blaise is the Patron Saint of Candle Makers.

"Okay, now it is your turn." He turned to Howard.

Howard looked a little put out by having to go first but he took a deep breath. "My name is Howard and I'm a member of Saint Nicholas dorm."

"I'm Charlie and I, too, am in Saint Nicholas."

"Charlie?" Father Blaise repeated as he thought to himself. "You wouldn't happen to be the Master Charlie MacCready the whole Abbey has been talking about these past few weeks, are you?"

Charlie could feel his face redden as all eyes turned toward him. He nodded quickly and hoped Father Blaise would move on.

"Well, I'm happy to meet you," he beamed. "Such a brave boy you are. How about this young man?"

Everyone looked at Dale as he struggled to say his name.

"M-m-my n-n-name is st-st-stutter d-d-dale," laughed Travis to which Dougary and Kenneth joined in.

Dale's cheeks turned red and he looked at Howard, Charlie and Gus as though for help.

"Master Bleckinger, that will cost you one afternoon in work crew," Father Blaise said coldly just as Howard opened his mouth to speak. "And let that be a warning to the rest of you. I will not tolerate making fun of each other in my class."

"Now, you, young man?" Father Blaise looked at Kenneth.

"My name is Kenneth J. DeVries, the Third. As you can see," he said as he boastfully displayed his new purple surplice, "I'm a member of Saint Peter dorm."

Dougary stood up next to his stool. Charlie was sure it was in an attempt to look more important since no one else stood up.

"My name is Dougary. I'm a member of Saint Peter dorm and, as of last year, a member of the Altar Boys Club."

"I'm Gus," Gus spoke up quickly. "I'm from Saint Nicholas dorm."

"I'm pleased to meet all of you," Father Blaise said, walking over to the chalkboard. "Now, let us begin. Contrary to what you may think, candle making is a very serious matter. It is an art. And I must say that Abbot Ambrose and the Abbey have come to rely on the sales of our candles as a serious source of income. Our candles have become famous for their quality as well as their beauty, and it's a real challenge to keep up with the order demands. As I mentioned earlier, we sell out each year at Oktoberfest, and our gift shop is constantly being restocked. If that weren't enough, we are looking into doing a mail-order venture, and possibly marketing them in some of the shops in town all year round. What skills you learn here will greatly help our Abbey, and will be useful to you later in life."

"I doubt that," Dougary whispered, half under his breath, but loud enough for everyone to hear.

"Master Duggan." Father Blaise fixed his gaze sternly on Dougary. "I am quite well aware of your reputation around here. And if you would like to join Master Bleckinger in work crew, it can be arranged."

"No, Father," Dougary said quietly.

Howard and Charlie glanced at each other as they stifled their laughter. Their pleased expressions did not go unnoticed by Dougary. He just sat on his stool and glared at them.

"Please open your books to page one and we will begin our lesson with the basic rolled beeswax candle," Father Blaise instructed. "Master Kugele, will you be so kind as to begin reading aloud to the class?"

The room was silent as Gus read. Dougary, Travis and Kenneth were uncharacteristically quiet, which Charlie found to be just as distracting.

After Gus finished reading the first lesson, Father Blaise closed his book. "What do you say we take a five minute stretching break? While you all go outside, I'll set up for our first candle project."

The boys wasted no time in getting outside. Howard and Charlie waited by the door for Gus and Dale, while keeping an eye on Dougary, Travis and Kenneth, who headed toward the swimming pool.

"Gus, you wanna come with us?" Howard invited.

The look on Gus's face said he did not but he shrugged and went along anyway. When they reached a grassy spot in the sun, they stopped, pulled up their cassocks and sat down.

"So, what's the story with that Kenneth guy?" Howard asked, trying not to look at Gus.

Gus shrugged.

"I mean does anyone know why he's here? He's obviously a resident since the students aren't due back for eight weeks," Howard reasoned.

"I'm not spying for you guys," Gus snapped defensively.

"No one is asking you to. We're just curious is all. Is he a good guy?" Howard quickly explained.

Gus thought for a moment, eyeing each of the boys suspiciously. Then his expression seemed to relax.

"Well, all I know is that he comes from a wealthy family. When he was ten, his father died from cancer. His mother and sister were both killed in a car accident last year. That's all I know."

Charlie gave Howard a curious look. Howard shook his head and smiled at Gus.

"Wow, nice work. You must be spending a lot of time with him."

"We've talked some, so what?"

"Nothing. I'm glad you have someone to talk to," Howard said. He glanced up just in time to see Dougary and his goons heading toward them. "Oh, great," he sighed and jumped to his feet. The others did the same. "Speaking of the devil. Brace yourselves, here they come."

"Hello, ladies," Dougary greeted in his usual snide manner.

"What do you want, dog breath?" Howard snapped.

"Oh, nothing," Dougary said acting very smug. "Just thought you might want to know break is over, and don't be late for class."

Howard was just about to snap at Dougary when Father Blaise stuck his head out the doorway and signaled to them all that it was time to return to class. Charlie rushed Howard, Gus and Dale back into the studio before anyone said another word.

Immediately when they all entered the room, they noticed sheets of yellowish wax lying on the table in front of their stools. It had the unmistakable pattern of a honeycomb and a faint scent of honey; at least Charlie thought he could smell it. On the table beside the wax were a bottle of scent crystals and three spools of various sizes of wick. Charlie took his seat.

"The trick to working with beeswax," Father Blaise reminded them, "is to use just enough pressure to hold your candle together and yet not so much that you ruin the honeycomb pattern." Father Blaise began pacing around the table and looking over the shoulders of the boys. "To start with, you will need to measure your wick. First, with the rulers I've supplied, measure the width of your sheet of beeswax. Good," he smiled, nodding as he watched them following his instructions. "Now you need to add a half an inch. In choosing the appropriate thickness of wick you need to consider the size of the candle you are making. For skinny candles you would use a thinner wick and for fatter candles, a heavier wick. Don't be afraid to consult your textbook for help."

Charlie glanced across the table at Gus. He looked a bit worried as he became tangled in an unraveling spool of wick. When Dale tried to help him, Gus pulled away and knocked over his bowl of crystals, scattering them all over the table. Impatiently, Howard reached across the table and grabbed the tangled wick from Gus. He snipped off a length of it and tossed it in front of Gus. He quickly balled up the remaining wick and set it down in the center of the table. Gus quickly scooped up the crystals and returned them to his bowl.

"Now, place the wick along the edge of your wax that is nearest to you." Father Blaise continued his instructions as he walked slowly around the table, seemingly oblivious to the commotion. He paused for a moment behind Kenneth and watched him to be sure he was following the instructions before moving on to Dougary and the rest of the boys. "Very good. This next part begins the most critical step. Carefully, turn the edge of your wax over the wick and crimp it tightly. Remember the example in your lesson book, not too much pressure. Now, take your small spoon and sprinkle a small line of scent crystals the length of your candle."

Charlie watched Howard to see how he did it. Then he copied.

"Very good," Father Blaise commended them while he scanned the table. "Okay, now slowly, gently, begin to roll your candle, keeping the wax tight while keeping a careful eye on your pressure. You don't want to harm the honeycomb pattern."

Charlie frowned as he stared intently at his candle, rolling it carefully, slowly. He did not notice Father Blaise behind him, looking over his shoulder. Father Blaise smiled and continued around the table.

"Oh, darn it," Gus sighed, and threw his hands in the air.

"What's the matter, now?" Howard asked, as Father Blaise stepped beside Gus.

"I ruined it. I knew I would. I pressed too hard," Gus lamented.

"Oh, don't fret it," Father Blaise laughed lightly. "You are doing a good job. Keep rolling, but not so hard."

"Ha! I'm finished," Travis laughed and held up his candle. With an inch of wick sticking out of the pointed end and a clump of crystals rolled up in its center, it resembled a snake after being fed more than a candle. "Whadaya think?"

Charlie looked at Travis, then at Father Blaise. Father Blaise's eyes widened, and the muscles in his jaw tightened. He walked over and snatched the unevenly rolled stick of wax from Travis's hand. "I think you need to take this a bit more seriously." Charlie ducked his head, hearing the anger in Father Blaise's tone. "To begin with, you are using too much pressure and you are not paying attention to keeping your candle even. This is not a race." He slammed the roll of wax back on the table.

Travis picked it up. "Well, I think it looks great," he

mockingly praised himself, then looked at Dougary and snickered.

Dougary shook his head and returned to slowly rolling his candle. Travis reached across the table with his long, unevenly rolled candle. He brushed the wick lightly against Dougary's cheek. Dougary jumped and let out a yell. His half-rolled candle fell onto the dusty floor as his stool toppled over, sending him crashing to the floor.

Father Blaise turned sharply and looked at Dougary. His eyes squinted and his lips tightened as he saw the candle wax covered in dust in Dougary's hands. He walked over to Dougary and grabbed the stool from the floor.

"Master Duggan," he said with clenched teeth. "You have been warned."

"But—" he started to protest, and scowled at Travis.

"Don't defend yourself!" Father Blaise snapped. "I don't want to hear excuses. This may be a joke to the both of you—yes, I'm talking to you too, Master Bleckinger—but this is a very serious matter. Your candles will be sold to help support the Monastery, and inevitably each of you. You have both earned yourselves an hour of work crew! I suggest you not waste any more of the wax, unless you want to spend every free moment this summer with me cleaning."

Dougary sat back down on his stool and placed his candle on the table in front of him. He gently dusted it off with his hands, pausing briefly to glare at Travis.

When their eyes met, Travis mouthed a word of apology but Dougary looked away. Travis looked at his deformed candle in front of him. Charlie thought for a moment he saw a bit of regret in Travis's expression. Carefully Travis began to unroll his candle and straighten it.

Father Blaise walked around the table, placing an empty

shoebox in front of the boys.

"Now each of you, use a marker and write your name on the end of your box. If there is already a name on the box, cross it off. You will keep your candles in your box and at the end of the day, I will examine your work and you will receive your grade."

Charlie looked at his shoebox and saw the name Ted Wilson scribbled its end. He crossed it off and wrote his name.

For the next two hours, the boys silently worked, filling their shoeboxes with candles. Even though it was not a competition, Charlie counted his candles and looked at Howard.

"How many do you have?"

"Ten. How about you?"

"The same."

The distant sound of the bell tolling noon caused everyone to look up at the clock hanging on the wall above Father Blaise's desk.

"That will be all for today," Father Blaise announced. "Before you leave, please bring your boxes to me. After I go through them, you may be dismissed. Tomorrow, we will work on more beeswax candles, so be punctual!"

Quickly the boys grabbed their boxes and formed a line in front of Father Blaise's desk. Dougary, Travis and Kenneth elbowed their way to the front of the line.

Charlie watched Father Blaise take the candles out of Dougary's box one at a time and examine them. He gently placed several into a larger box beside his desk and returned three to Dougary's shoe box.

"Very good work, Master Duggan. These are not up to the standard of quality the Abbey needs for its booth. You may have them."

When Travis stepped forward, he reluctantly surrendered

his box. Father Blaise looked inside and at Travis. The expression on his face told all that needed to be said.

"A little less horsing around and more paying attention, I think are needed here. Am I clear, Master Bleckinger?"

"Yes, Father."

Kenneth stepped forward and handed his box over for inspection.

"Is this supposed to be funny?" Father Blaise asked, and looked directly at Kenneth. "What did you do to these?" He picked up the six candles, all smashed together in one clump. "You will get an F for the day, and you have earned yourself two hours of work crew with me this Saturday. You are dismissed, Master DeVries."

Once through the line, Charlie, Howard and Dale waited outside for Gus. When he finally appeared, he was holding one candle in his fist.

"Wow!" Howard praised. "You must be a pro at this."

Gus looked at his friends unfazed. "What do I need with a stupid old candle?" Before anyone could stop him, he threw the candle into the woods.

"Why did you do that?" Howard asked.

"If you want it, go get it," Gus answered.

"What's going on? I thought you did great?"

"I did, but a lot of good it does me. I'm still stuck here with all of you losers."

"Gus!" Charlie gasped. Gus just ignored him and headed off to the Abbey alone.

"We need to talk to Prior Emmanuel the minute he gets back," Charlie said, turning toward Howard. "This is getting out of control."

"I don't understand it," Howard said, shaking his head. "Why did he do that?"

"Should I g-g-get the candle?" Dale asked.
"No," Howard answered. "Leave it. Let's go."

THE BURNING BUSH

The air smelled fresh and clean after the two-day rain. Charlie pulled up the hem of his cassock, holding it in his fist, while he and Howard made their way through the trees toward the candle studio. The ground felt soft under Charlie's feet. He tried to avoid the muddy spots but still worried his shoes were not as water resistant as he hoped.

"Slow down," he groaned while he followed after Howard.

"Keep your voice down," Howard hissed. "You don't want to alert Dougary and his goons, do you?"

"No," Charlie agreed. He still felt the sting from the pinecones Travis and Dougary pelted him with the other day when he used the path to get to class.

"Are you sure Prior Emmanuel is supposed to be back today?" Charlie asked, changing the subject.

"That's what Abbot Ambrose told me. But he said Prior Emmanuel will be leaving again. He has to take some of the monks to the Priory," Howard answered. "Funny, I didn't even know there *was* a Priory."

"How long before he leaves for there?"

"We—" Howard stopped so suddenly that Charlie bumped into him.

"What's the—" Charlie snapped, but noticed Howard staring at something ahead. He looked in front of them a few feet. "What do you think happened?"

"I don't know," Howard answered. He walked closer and crouched down. He stared at the blackened ground at the base of a tree truck. "It looks like someone set a bush on fire trying to burn this tree down."

"Why would someone want to do that? And when could they have done it? I mean, we've been coming this way every day this week and haven't noticed it before."

"Probably last night. Remember it rained really hard. Maybe it put the fire out before anyone noticed," Howard offered as an explanation and stood up. "Or maybe we just have missed it."

"Do you think we should tell Father Mark?"

"Yeah, you wait here, I'll go get him."

Before Charlie could protest, Howard ran off in the direction of the Abbey. Alone, Charlie began looking around the ground for some clue as to whom or what started the fire. Just when he was about to give up something caught his eye under a nearby fern. He crouched down to see what it was, careful not to get his cassock and surplice muddy. He recognized it right way and picked it up.

"It's just over here," Howard said as he led Father Mark, Brother Simon and Father Vicar off the path toward Charlie.

Panicked, Charlie stuffed the object into the pocket of his cassock and stood up.

"What were you boys doing out here?" Father Vicar asked the accusing tone evident in his voice.

"We were on our way to class," Howard explained.

"Shouldn't you be using the path?" Father Vicar continued.

Howard ignored him and turned to see what Father Mark and Brother Simon were doing. They were crouched down by the burnt ground and tree trunk examining it.

"Well we can thank heaven for the rain we had," Father Mark said while he stood up. "Otherwise this would have been much worse."

"Do you think it was an accident?"

"No, Master MacCready, this was no accident. I'm quite sure whoever set this was intending to have the whole forest go up in flames."

"Did you boys notice anyone in this area in the last couple days?" Brother Simon asked.

"No," Charlie and Howard said, shaking their heads.

"That's because we have the culprits right here," Father Vicar sneered.

"Oh, will you knock it off, Vicar," Brother Simon snapped. "I'm sure if Master MacCready or Master Miller set this fire they wouldn't be bringing it to our attention."

"How can you be so sure? It would be pretty clever of them to try to draw suspicion away from themselves. Let me go on record for saying I find it odd that ever since Master MacCready arrived he is always somehow connected to whatever trouble is going on," Father Vicar continued as he glared at Charlie.

"That's enough, Vicar," Father Mark said with a sigh of exasperation. "Are you boys sure you didn't see anyone in this area?

"No, Father," Howard answered, shaking his head.

"Then we'll take it from here. You better get off to class. You're already late and Father Blaise doesn't tolerate tardiness well. And boys, not a word of this to anyone."

"Yes, Father," they answered, and quickly headed off to

class. Charlie resisted the urge to look back but he was sure he could feel Father Vicar's icy stare.

When they reached the door of the candle studio, Charlie grabbed Howard's arm and took him aside.

"What?"

Charlie cringed at the loudness of Howard's voice.

"Will you keep your voice down?" he said, and thrust his hand into his pocket and pulled out the straw ribbon tied in a bow that he had found underneath the fern. He showed it to Howard.

"What's that?" he asked, staring indifferently at the piece of straw.

"Don't you recognize it?"

Howard frowned as he thought. Suddenly his eyes widened. "It's that stuff we use to tie around the candles isn't it?"

"Yes." Charlie said, nodding his head and wishing Howard would keep his voice down.

"Where did you find it?"

"It was by the burned bush," Charlie answered.

"You should show it Father Mark."

"And get Gus in trouble?"

"Gus? What's this have to do with him?"

"Don't you remember after our first class when Father Blaise let us keep one of our candles? Gus threw his candle over there," Charlie said, pointing in the direction of the burned bush.

"Oh yeah," Howard realized and looked back at the forest.

"So, I couldn't tell Father Mark because he would ask us more questions and we would have to tell him about Gus."

"You don't really think Gus did that, do you?" Howard asked.

"I don't want to," Charlie answered, ashamed of himself

for thinking his friend could actually be capable of such a deed.

"Well he didn't!" Howard snapped in a harsh whisper. "Why would he go back after that candle? He didn't want it in the first place, remember?"

Howard had a point, Charlie thought. Gus had thrown the candle away, why would he then go back and use it to try to start a fire.

"I guess you're right," he admitted. "I'm sorry."

"We better get in there before we get into more trouble," Howard said as he opened the door.

When the boys entered the studio, the class was huddled around the end of the table, watching Father Blaise as he poured hot wax into a large tub of sand. Almost as one, everyone looked up at them.

"Well, well," Father Blaise said as he finished pouring out the wax. "So nice of you boys to join us. You each have an hour of work crew beginning at the end of class today."

"But—" Howard started to protest.

"Don't defend yourself!" Father Blaise snapped. "I don't want to hear any excuses. I see that both of you appear to be breathing so you don't have any excuse for being tardy."

"We were with Father Mark," Howard blurted out quickly.

"That's two hours!" Father Blaise snapped. "Care to make it three?"

"No, Father. We're sorry, Father. It won't happen again," Charlie said, before Howard could make matters worse.

"Splendid," Father Blaise said, looking pleased with himself. "Now, Master DeVries, would you be so kind as to review for the benefit of our tardy pupils what we have been doing?"

"Yes, Father," Kenneth answered smugly.

As Kenneth explained how to make a sand candle, Charlie

tried to pay attention but found his mind wandering as he looked at the boys. Travis was grinning and making taunting faces at Howard and him. Charlie ignored him. On the other hand, Gus was listening intently, staring at the cooling wax in the sand.

"Now remember," Kenneth said as he finished his summation. "Sand candles allow your inner artist to come out. Sand candles are free-form. Limited only by your imagination, so let your imaginations go and enjoy, but don't forget your wick, and when you pour your wax into your sand mold, do it gently so you don't ruin your shapes."

"That is correct, Master DeVries. Thank you." Father Blaise applauded. "One more thing." Father Blaise looked directly at Dougary and Travis. "Anyone caught making obscene forms in the sand is automatic work crew. Is that clear?"

"Yes, Father Blaise," the two boys answered in unison.

The rest of the day seemed to drag on. In no time, Howard and Charlie caught on with the lesson. Taking note of the sample candle that Father Blaise showed the class, Charlie took a small bowl and pressed it into his damp sand. Then in the bottom he pressed his finger in the sand making four nubs for legs. He glanced beside him at Travis who was snickering while he buried his hand in the sand. Charlie did not need to see it to know that Travis was making an obscene gesture mold. He shook his head, deciding not to say anything, and let Travis hang himself again.

After the rest of the class had been dismissed for the day, Father Blaise turned his attention to Howard and Charlie.

"You can begin by cleaning off the table, dusting the shelves and sweeping the floor. Be careful around the sand tubs," he warned. "I'll be outside for a moment."

Howard grabbed the dust rags and threw Charlie one. As

soon as the door closed behind Father Blaise, Howard sat down on his stool.

"Of all of the rotten luck!" he sighed. "We'll never catch Prior Emmanuel before he leaves for the Priory."

"Maybe if we hurry and get done, Father Blaise will let us go," Charlie said as he swept the sand from the table onto the floor. Once he finished, he quickly ran the cloth over the wooden shelves, careful not to disturb the rows of candles.

"Are you gonna help?" Charlie asked.

Howard looked up at him from his seat at the table. "Yeah," he said.

By the time Father Blaise returned to the studio, Howard had finished with sweeping the floor. Father Blaise smiled.

"Very good, boys," he said and nodded. "Master MacCready, there are some empty boxes in the closet I would like you to bring out."

"Yes, Father," Charlie said. He opened the closet doors. Inside were stacks of long, narrow boxes with lids. "How many do you want?"

"Just bring two or three for now. I will show you both how to properly pack the candles to get them ready for shipping and for our booth."

Charlie brought the boxes over to the table and set them down. Howard's shoulders slumped as he looked at the clock, and realized Father Blaise was going to keep them the whole two hours.

THE DEATH KNELL

"I wish we could've talked to Prior Emmanuel last Friday. I'm really getting worried about Gus," Howard lamented as he and Charlie headed off to class. "All because of that stupid you-know-what. If Father Mark hadn't told us not to tell anyone about it, I'm sure Father Blaise would have understood."

"Well, nothing we can do about it now. But since you brought it up, have you heard anything more about it?" Charlie asked as they passed the grotto.

"Not a peep. Father Mark isn't like Abbot Ambrose. He never shares anything with me. How about you?"

"Nothing," Charlie sighed.

The two stopped when they came to the path to the studio. They looked around and seeing no one, decided it was safe to take it. They picked up their pace and in no time made it to the studio door.

"After class, I'll see if I can find out when Prior Emmanuel will be back," Charlie said and opened the door.

Howard glanced over his shoulder at Dougary and the rest. "Good."

As they took their seats at the table, they noticed an empty cafeteria tray set in front of each stool.

"What are these for?" Howard asked, looking curiously at Father Blaise.

"All in good time," he answered.

As soon as everyone arrived, Father Blaise stood up and walked over to the end of the table.

"Today we are going to make a different candle. This is one that I came up with years ago, so there isn't a book to tell you how it's done. You'll have to listen carefully. I call this candle the stacked wafer candle." He held up a candle made of half-inch thick squares of brightly colored wax stacked randomly on top of each other. The whole thing appeared to have been dipped into clear wax, sealing it.

Charlie looked around the table. Everyone appeared to be listening with the exception of Travis. He was already playing with a spool of wick. Father Blaise continued his instruction as he made his way over to Travis, an empty tray in hand. Without warning, he smacked Travis in the back of the head with it, not enough to hurt him but enough to get his attention.

"Now, pay attention, Master Bleckinger," he snapped.

"This is going to be a team effort. There are seven of you, so each of you will make a different color. I've already put the wax dye you will use in front of you. There is to be no fighting. Once you have melted your wax and poured it into your tray, you will be done for the day."

A collective gasp of excitement rose from all around the table. The boys wasted no time retrieving their melting pots from the shelf and breaking off chucks of wax. When everyone was ready, Father Blaise flipped the switch on the wall by his desk providing power to the hot plates. Charlie watched the wax begin to melt in his pot.

"Remember, safety first," Father Blaise said. "I don't want

anyone getting burned." He walked around the table, looking over the shoulders of his pupils, watching their progress. "Make sure you use enough dye to get a rich hue. There is no need to rush."

"How's this, Father?" Dougary asked, and poured a spoonful of wax onto his tray.

"Very nice, very nice indeed, Master Duggan. You may begin pouring."

"What about mine?" Kenneth spoke up next.

"Master DeVries, how many times do I have to tell you, don't be afraid to use more color. Here," Father Blaise grabbed the bottle of dye and poured it directly into Kenneth's melting pot. "Now stir it up," he instructed.

Kenneth, his face red with embarrassment, did as he was told. He poured a test spoonful onto his tray.

"See, how brilliant that is? You may begin pouring."

"Father, how's this?" Howard asked.

Before Father Blaise could answer, the Abbey's bell began to toll. Father Blaise froze and looked up toward the ceiling. Crossing himself, he looked at the boys with a concerned expression. Charlie glanced at the clock on the wall, then turned to Howard.

Howard cocked his head and listened to the slow, steady ringing. His face suddenly went pale and he looked at Charlie. "It's the death knell," he whispered.

Father Blaise walked over to his desk and flipped the master switch, shutting off the hot plates. He turned back around and looked at the boys.

"Leave everything where it is. Class is dismissed. You should all return to your dorms immediately."

Quietly, the boys did as they were instructed. Even Travis behaved until he was outside.

Charlie did not wait around. He raced up the hill toward the Abbey after Howard. Mentally he counted the tolling of the bell. When it stopped, the boys stopped.

Howard turned around and looked at Charlie, a puzzled look on his face.

"The bell tolls once for every year of the dead monk's life, right?" Charlie asked as he caught his breath.

"Yes." Howard nodded.

"Have you been counting?"

"Yes," Howard answered. "But there must be a mistake. It's impossible. I only counted nineteen."

"Same here," Charlie concurred. "But that would mean it was one of the new postulants or novices."

"I know," Howard answered just as the tolling started up again. "Wha—Come on, let's find Father Mark."

Charlie followed Howard through the main doors of the Abbey and into the student wing, the shortest route to Father Mark's office. When they entered the hall, they noticed Abbot Ambrose and Father Mark standing outside their offices. Abbot Ambrose looked up, then turned sharply and disappeared into his office, closing the door behind him. Father Mark looked at the boys and waited for them to approach.

"You boys should be in your dorm," his voice cracking as he spoke. "Off with you now," he added firmly then disappeared into his office and closed the door.

Howard turned around and looked at Charlie. "This isn't good. Come on."

Saint Nicholas dorm was eerily quiet. Each boy sat on his bed listening to the tolling bell. Howard sat leaning against the headboard of his bed with his arms wrapped around his pillow. Charlie sat staring out the window at the blue sky counting in an undertone to himself.

Abruptly, the tolling stopped again.

Charlie looked at Howard. "How many this time?"

"Twenty-two."

"Who's twenty-two?"

"No one I know."

"They only ring the bells for members of the Abbey, don't they?" Charlie asked.

Just then the bells began to toll again. Charlie returned to counting. Some of the other boys walked out of their cubicles and huddled around the sofa and chairs in the lounge area. All silently listened to the somber tolling.

"I don't understand it," said Charlie growing anxious and shaking his head. "Surely they wouldn't keep ringing that bell for— Listen. It stopped. How many this time?"

"Forty-five, I think." Howard shook his head. "I can't count anymore. I wish someone would tell us what's going on. This is driving me crazy."

The dormitory doors opened and Gus walked into the room. He headed straight for Howard and Charlie's cubicle. His face was red and his eyes and cheeks were damp with tears.

"What is it?" Charlie asked, being the first to see him.

Gus just shook his head and looked at them.

"This is crazy," Howard said, sounding exasperated. He threw his pillow aside and stood up. "Four tolls mean four monks." Suddenly his eyes widened, as though a thought had just occurred to him. He brushed past Gus and headed for the door.

Charlie jumped up and followed him. "Howard, what? What's going on?" Charlie asked.

Howard paused when he reached the doors, and turned around. "I don't know. Stay here, I'll be right back." He pushed through the doors and was gone.

Charlie turned back to Gus.

"Do you know what's going on?"

Gus did not say a word. His expression slowly changed to an angry glare. Without a word he stormed out of the dorm.

"Honestly, can the day get any worse?" Charlie sighed and dropped down into Howard's favorite chair in the lounge.

With the tolling over, the other boys began to come to life. Though not as noisy as usual, they began talking and milling about the dorm, anxious to be allowed out.

Charlie slumped in the chair, resting his elbows on its arms and pressing his palms over his ears. He was not trying to block out the noise from the others. He was trying to silence his noisy thoughts. His mind kept asking question after question but giving him no answers. He wondered where Howard had gone and why he was not back yet. What was the matter with Gus? Did he know something? Why did he run out? Where did he go?

The dormitory doors opened. Charlie jumped to his feet. Howard entered followed closely by Brother Simon and Abbot Ambrose.

Charlie studied his great-uncle's eyes. They were red and damp with tears. A sudden sinking feeling came over him. He looked at Howard to give him a clue. Howard did not look back. He plopped down into his chair and avoided eye contact with everyone.

"Boys," Brother Simon called out in a gentler tone, most unusual for him. "Please gather around and have a seat."

As soon as everyone was present and seated, Abbot Ambrose stepped forward. Brother Simon stood behind Howard and put a firm hand on Howard's shoulder as though bracing him for what was to come.

"Let me begin by saying, all classes are canceled for the rest of the next week," Abbot Ambrose began. "For those of you who are members of the Altar Boys Club there will be a meeting first thing after breakfast tomorrow morning." He paused as he looked at their faces.

"As you are all well aware from the tolling of the bell, our Abbey has suffered a great loss today. There is no easy way to say this and for that I'm sorry. On their way back to the Abbey, there was a car accident. Postulants Armando, Enrique, Novice Stephen and Prior Emmanuel were all killed."

A sudden, collective gasp followed by muffled sobbing filled the dorm. Brother Simon tightened his grip on Howard's shoulder as Howard lowered his head and cried. Abbot Ambrose appeared visibly shaken. He knelt down next to Charlie and put his arm around his shoulders. "It's okay," he whispered tenderly as tears streamed down Charlie's cheeks. He looked around the dorm at the other boys. Slowly he stood up.

"For the rest of the evening the brothers will be in prayer. I would ask that you observe silence when you are in the building and if you must go outdoors, please keep the noise down to a respectful level. If you have any questions, please direct them to your prefects. Let us say a prayer. You may stay seated."

After the prayer, the boys sat in stunned silence while the Abbot left.

"Please get ready for the noon meal," Brother Simon instructed gently, not in his usual cold, militaristic manner. "Afterward we will meet back here and I'll do my best to answer your questions. Masters Miller and MacCready, I would like to speak with you in the hallway."

Silently the two followed Brother Simon into the hall. Stopping away from the doorway, Brother Simon turned to them.

"At today's meals, since the brothers will be in prayer, I

will need the two of you to be servers for your table."

"Okay," Howard answered. "We can do it."

Brother Simon looked at Charlie who still appeared to be quite shaken by the news of the deaths.

"Master MacCready?"

Charlie looked at him. He heard what Brother Simon said.

"Are you okay?" Brother Simon asked.

"Yes, Brother," Charlie said, though his voice was a bit shaky. "I'm okay. Howard and I can do it."

Brother Simon straightened his back, making him appear to grow taller right before their eyes.

"Very well, then," he said in his usual icy tone. "Go down to the kitchen at once. The boys from the other dorms will be meeting there for instructions from Sister Anthony." With that, Brother Simon turned around and left them.

The refectory was eerily quiet when Charlie and Howard entered. Much to their surprise and dismay, Dougary and Kenneth were pressed into service for Saint Peter dorm. The other boys from Saint Thomas and Saint Sebastian dorm stood by their tables.

When Sister Anthony entered the refectory from the kitchen, it was obvious that she had been crying. Not wanting to upset her further, the boys listened carefully while she explained their duties.

After Grace was said, Charlie and Howard quickly made their rounds and took their seats at the table. Gus was quiet and focused on his lunch. Charlie leaned forward.

"So, what happened to you this afternoon?"

Gus did not look up. He continued to stuff a slice of gravy-soaked biscuit into his mouth.

"Gus," Charlie said a bit louder.

Gus looked up, his cheeks bulging. "What?" he said plainly

annoyed.

"We just want to know where you went this afternoon," Howard spoke up.

"It's none of your business where I went," Gus snapped and returned to eating his lunch.

Charlie looked at Howard.

The rest of the meal passed quietly and the boys returned to their dorm afterward. Howard sat in his usual seat facing the doors. Charlie and Gus sat at opposite ends of the sofa with two of the smaller boys between them. No one said a word, and everyone jumped when the doors opened.

Brother Simon entered the dorm, his back perfectly straight, shoulders back, head held rigid and high. The look on his face was his usual stoic stare. He walked to the center of the lounge and looked down his nose at them. For a moment, Charlie thought he saw a glimpse of emotion in Brother Simon's eyes.

"I imagine you boys have questions," Brother Simon began. "I will do my best to answer them."

Howard raised his hand.

"Master Miller?"

"What happened? I mean, there are car accidents all of the time and people survive."

Brother Simon's shoulders dipped slightly and his eyes became shiny with tears. For a split second, Charlie saw it again, the caring prefect, then it vanished.

"Early this morning, Prior Emmanuel and Novice Stephen, along with the two new novices from our Priory, headed back to the Abbey. Prior Emmanuel was anxious to get back home," Brother Simon said coldly, as though he was reporting the evening news. "They had only come about a third of the way when a semi-truck passing another forced them off the road. The car struck the guard rail and rolled down a slope into a river."

One of the boys seated next to Charlie gasped, and began to cry. Brother Simon's hands moved beneath his robes and the look flashed again in his eyes, but only for a second. Charlie put his arm around the boy's shoulders and quietly hushed him.

"Who was driving?" came the next question. Charlie recognized the voice and looked up.

"Who was driving?" Gus asked again a bit bolder.

"Why does it matter?" Brother Simon answered and cocked his head.

"I need to know, that's all."

"Prior Emmanuel was driving."

"Did the semi driver stop to help?" Gus fired back another question.

"As I understand, yes, he stopped. He radioed for help," Brother Simon answered, looking intently at Gus with what appeared to be a look of concern and confusion.

Gus looked away to avoid looking at their prefect.

"Several cars stopped to help. One of the drivers jumped into the river to try to save our brothers. According to police, the car was upside down. The windows on the passenger side had been shattered possibly on impact, but the brother nearest the door didn't make it. The Good Samaritan who dove in freed Prior Emmanuel and brought him to the surface. But it was too late when he went back under to get the others," he explained.

"So Prior Emmanuel survived?" Howard asked sounding hopeful.

Brother Simon shook his head. "No, Master Miller. He was already gone."

"Did they suffer?" another boy asked.

Brother Simon looked at him. "I'm sorry, I don't know." Again, the look and it was gone. "From what I have been told by one in the medical field, drowning is a painless way to die."

Howard scoffed under his breath. "How do they know," he murmured. "They're still alive."

Brother Simon pretended not to hear. "If there are no further questions, let us all kneel and say a prayer." Brother Simon took the string of beads that hung from the pocket of his habit and led them in prayer.

~§~

Charlie was relieved when it was finally time for lights out. He lay on his back in his bed, staring at the ceiling, unable to sleep. He turned and looked across the small cubicle at Howard. Howard lay on his side, facing the partition with his back to Charlie. Even in the dim moonlight that shone through the large window above Charlie's bed, Charlie could tell Howard was crying. Slowly, Charlie turned over and looked out the window. The glow of the moon shone on the Great Lawn below. Suddenly, a movement caught his attention. He strained his eyes to see what was down there. Though four stories up, Charlie could tell it was his great-uncle walking alone. Charlie watched him for a moment, then quietly slipped back down in his bed. He looked up at the glowing moon. A strange yet vaguely familiar feeling rose in his chest. It was the same sense of deep sadness he felt when his grandfather died over two years ago. Tears filled his eyes. He rolled over and buried his face in his pillow.

~§~

The afternoon sun was hot against his black cassock as Charlie walked across the Great Lawn after lunch with Howard and Dale.

"You know, it's been four days already. When are the serving brothers coming back? I hate having to wait on everyone," Howard complained.

"I bet Father Mark's going to make us permanent servers from now on," Charlie said, stopping beside one of the many ponds dotting the front grounds. He pulled up his cassock, exposing his blue jeans beneath, and sat down on the grass. Howard and Dale did the same. Mindlessly, Howard began to pull at the grass in front of him while he stared at the shimmering water in the pond.

"You really th-th-think he will?" Dale asked.

Charlie shrugged his shoulders and nodded that he did.

"I still can't believe he's dead, they're all dead," Howard said, changing the subject.

"M-m-me neither," Dale added.

"I know Brother Simon said drowning was a painless way to die, but I still think it would be awful. I mean, not being able to breathe. I wonder what they were thinking? Did they know they were going to die?" Charlie asked while he stared at the goldfish swimming beneath the surface of the pond.

"I don't think they had time to think anything," Howard answered. "I tried seeing how long I could hold my breath underwater yesterday while in the pool. I could only do it a few seconds, not even long enough to think of opening a window or anything." He threw a handful of grass at the water. "I wish Brother Simon didn't tell us. I mean, being in a car accident is bad enough. I can't get the image of all of them being trapped inside the car. Their habits soaked and heavy, weighing them down even more as they struggled to get out. Then—"

"Thanks, Howard. That really helps," Charlie said while he stood up. "I have to walk or do something. I can't just sit here."

Just then, the sound of an approaching car touched their ears. They all turned their heads toward the sound as a black hearse came into view. It was followed by another and still two more. They moved slowly along the narrow two-lane road that bordered the west edge of the Great Lawn toward the Abbey. Howard and Dale jumped to their feet and the three stood, watching in silence. When the last hearse passed in front of them, they headed back across the lawn to the Abbey.

They stopped in the shadow of a tree and watched. One-by-one the hearses pulled forward and stopped. Six monks stepped forward with the hoods of their habits pulled over their heads, hiding their faces from view. The back door of the hearse was opened and the six monks pulled out a plain wooden coffin. Abbot Ambrose stood back, watching and blessing each casket when the brothers paused in front of him. The brothers then carried the casket to the top of the stairs where a casket stand on wheels waited. When the next hearse pulled forward, the process was repeated with six other monks.

Once all four of the caskets were at the top of the stairs, the brothers slowly, solemnly took them into the Abbey Church. Charlie could not help but wonder which casket held the body of his friend and former sacristan Stephen, and which held Prior Emmanuel.

"We better go get ready for the funeral," Howard said when the last hearse drove away. "We'll see you later, Dale."

"O-k-k-kay."

The sacristy, "the priest's dressing room," as Stephen called it when Charlie became an Altar Boy, was crowded. Abbot Ambrose and three other visiting priests were donning their vestments. In the separate room beyond the main sacristy, the Altar Boys gathered and made their preparations. Charlie picked up the gold-plated processional cross and took his place at the head of the line. He looked over his shoulder at Howard who stood, back straight, holding an ornate golden candlestick holder and coaxing the wick to keep burning. Charlie nodded silently to himself and turned back around.

It's strange how everyone appeared calm, no tears, no sad faces, just business as usual, Charlie thought. Then he wondered why?

Father Mark stepped into the doorway between the two rooms. "We're ready boys," he announced quietly.

Slowly Charlie led the group of Altar Boys into the main sacristy out the back door. Today they would walk around the outside of the Abbey to the front entrance where they would join all the monks of the Abbey.

Two men held the large wooden doors into the Abby Church open. Charlie ignored them. He focused his eyes on the altar in the sanctuary, just beyond the four caskets draped in white linen cloths. He tried not to think of Prior Emmanuel and Stephen and kept silently telling himself, you can do this.

While the organist played, Charlie led the procession up the center aisle. Howard and Gus followed one step behind him, careful to keep their candles burning. Dougary, his face clouded by the burning incense, coughed and swung the thurible away from him but kept pace behind.

Once he reached the sanctuary, Charlie took his place in the center, in front of the altar and turned around to face the congregation. Howard and Gus stood silently on either side of him. He watched the monks walk past the coffins and take their stations in the choir stalls on either side of the sanctuary. He wondered if they felt as strange inside as he did.

When Abbot Ambrose, who was at the end of the procession, reached the sanctuary he took the incense boat from Dougary. Dougary opened the thurible and grimaced while

Abbot Ambrose spooned more incense onto the burning ember. A white cloud bellowed up in Dougary's face. Charlie stifled his grin.

Abbot Ambrose handed Dougary the incense boat and took the thurible from him. His lips moved while he said a silent prayer and walked around each casket swinging the thurible. Charlie stifled a cough when the Abbot passed in front of him.

The Mass seemed to go on longer than usual to Charlie. He sat between Howard and Gus on the side of the sanctuary and watched the other altar boys do their assigned tasks.

Finally, the Mass was over. Charlie was relieved that they did not have to do the normal procession from the Abbey to the cemetery chapel. With the four caskets, the chapel was too small to hold them the traditional three days before the burial. "It has something to do with Jesus and the three days he spent in the tomb," Stephen had explained when Prior Anselm died two years ago. Charlie still did not understand, but was still happy this part of the day was over.

Right after the funeral, the Abbot Ambrose and the monastery hosted the families of the novices and Prior Emmanuel at a buffet gathering on the back lawn. The monks had worked hard over the last few days erecting a canopy over what used to be the boys' baseball field. Once outside, Charlie spotted Howard getting himself a glass of punch. He made his way through the small crowd until he reached the table.

"How are you doing?" Charlie asked.

"I'm just glad it's over. You see Gus?"

"Not since he put his candle away. Why?" Charlie asked looking over his shoulder at the crowd.

"I don't know," Howard said. "Ever since we heard the news about Prior Emmanuel, he's been disappearing by himself. I'm worried."

"You don't think he's up to something do you?"

Howard made a half-snarl, half-concerned face. "I don't know. I was counting on Prior Emmanuel to help us get through to him. Now I don't know what to do or worse, what Gus will do."

"You have a point," Charlie agreed and poured himself some punch.

"So, how are you doing?" Howard asked, gulping down the last of his punch and going back for another ladleful.

"Me? I'm okay. Why?" Charlie answered.

"I was watching you during the funeral. You and Stephen were friends, or at least it appeared that way."

"Yeah, we were sort of," Charlie shrugged. "He used to give me a bad time now and again. Remember?"

"Yeah."

That night, after lights out, Charlie lay awake in his bed. He could not sleep. He tried listening to the sounds of the other boys slow breathing, hoping it would lull him to sleep but he could not stop thinking about Prior Emmanuel and Stephen. Quietly he slipped out of his bed. He put on his bathrobe and found himself walking back to the Abbey Church.

When he opened the heavy door a sliver of light from behind him raced across the floor into the nave of the church. Quickly Charlie stepped inside and closed the door letting the light retreat back into the foyer. Quietly, he slipped into the back pew. He sat, staring at the four draped coffins.

A solitary candle on a tall gold-plated pole stood at the head of each coffin. Their flames, the only light in the church, cast eerie shadows and made the statues along the outer walls appear to move. Charlie pulled his legs up to his chest and wrapped his arms around them. He rested his chin on his knees.

"Why?" he whispered out loud.

Slowly, Abbot Ambrose stepped from the shadows and made his way to the center aisle. Charlie watched him intently. The Abbot walked down the aisle, his footsteps echoing off the tall walls, until he came to the pew where Charlie sat. He turned around facing the altar and genuflected before sitting down beside Charlie.

"Son," he spoke softly patting Charlie's knee.

Charlie instantly put his feet back on the floor and sat up.

"Shouldn't you be in bed? Lights out was three hours ago."

"I'm sorry, Father," Charlie answered. "But I couldn't sleep. I can't stop thinking about Stephen. I can't believe they're gone. I spoke with him before he left on their Retreat. He was looking forward to making his vows and serving God as a monk. He gave me a hug and told me he'd be back soon. That's what my parents told my grandma, and they never came back either. Father, do you think they're dead?"

Abbot Ambrose looked at Charlie. "Who?" he asked.

"My parents," Charlie whispered, fearing if he said the words too loudly it would make it true.

"I can't answer that, son," Abbot Ambrose sighed. "But I do know this; you should never doubt their love for you."

"Yeah," Charlie said, sounding less than reassured. "May I tell you something?"

"Of course, you may," Abbot Ambrose answered, and playfully nudged Charlie with his shoulder.

"You won't think badly of me, will you?"

"Well, that all depends."

"I don't miss them, my parents, I mean," Charlie said thoughtfully. "I mean, I don't really *know* them. I know *about* them from stories Grandma told me, but that's not the same as actually knowing them, is it?"

"Charlie, just because you can't see a person doesn't mean

you can't know them, love them or even miss them," Abbot Ambrose said softly. "For example, we know God from what we see around us and from what is written in the Bible and we can't see Him but we still love him, don't we?"

"Well, yeah. I mean, yes," Charlie corrected himself.

"So, from everything you've been told about your parents, you can still know them and it is okay for you to love them and even miss them."

"But sometimes it hurts really bad," Charlie said, rubbing his chest through his clothes.

"I know, son." Abbot Ambrose nodded and put his arm around Charlie's shoulders, giving him a gentle hug.

The two of them sat silently, staring blindly at the row of caskets. Charlie yawned.

"Well, I think it's time you found your way back to your dorm and bed. Morning will come early and classes are resuming," Abbot Ambrose instructed.

"Okay," Charlie agreed. He stood up and stepped past his great-uncle. He genuflected and turned around. "Thank you, Father Abbot."

"You are welcome, son. Good night."

Charlie walked to the back of the church and paused as he reached the doors. He turned back just as the Abbot reached the front where the row of caskets sat. Quietly, Charlie backed away from the doors, into the shadows. He watched Abbot Ambrose stop at the foot of the casket on the left, his hands smoothing the linen shroud.

"Well, Em," Abbot Ambrose spoke in a hoarse whisper. "You never did want to be Prior but you didn't have to leave us like this. Now what am I to do? I need you, Em. You're my right arm, my strength and most of all my best friend."

As Abbot Ambrose's quiet sobs touched Charlie's ears,

Charlie thought of Howard. Quietly he slipped out the side door and headed back to his dorm.

THE MAP

The afternoon sun shone through the window of Father Cecil's room, warming the side of his face while he sat in his corner chair. His fingers glided over the raised bumps on the pages of the odd-looking Bible while his lips silently formed words. He stopped and turned his ear toward Charlie who was busy dusting the lamp and table. Nodding to himself, he pulled the ribbon marker across the page and closed the book.

"Okay, Charlie, what's bothering you?"

Charlie turned around and gave him a puzzled look. "Nothing," he answered with a shrug.

"Charlie, I can tell when something's wrong. I'm blind, not deaf, remember? I can hear you sighing as you breathe. So, stop fiddling with that dust rag and have a seat."

Charlie froze for a second and looked at the twisted rag in his hands. He sat down in the chair, convinced that while Father Cecil was blind, he was also psychic.

"I'm just thinking, that's all," Charlie said.

"Thinking about?"

"Father, I need to confess something."

"Oh? Are you asking me to hear your Confession?"

"No!" Charlie blurted. "I mean, not that I wouldn't want you to but, I mean...I didn't mean it that way."

"That's okay. What is it?" Father Cecil chuckled.

"It's been three weeks and I'm still thinking about the accident," Charlie admitted. "I feel sort of strange inside."

"Oh?" Father Cecil said, tilting his head and staring straight ahead. "Like what?"

"I don't know. I just can't stop thinking about Brother Stephen. The only people I know who've died were my grandpa and Prior Anselm, but they were old. Brother Stephen wasn't a whole lot older than me."

"That's true."

"I don't understand why it bothers me."

Father Cecil smiled understandingly. "We all handle loss in different ways. Some cry. Some internalize their feelings. It's all part of what is called the grieving process. There is no right or wrong way to grieve."

"But when my Grandpa died, it didn't feel like this," Charlie admitted. He put his hand to his chest and disturbed the key and medal beneath his cassock.

"What was that?" Father Cecil asked.

"What was what?"

"That metal 'tink' sound?"

"You heard that?"

"I'm blind, not—"

"Deaf," Charlie finished. "It's something my Grandma gave me the day I came here."

"What is it?" Father Cecil asked holding out his hand in Charlie's direction.

Charlie knew the gesture and stood up. He pulled the chain from beneath his collar and with it came his treasures.

Leaving the chain securely around his neck and holding onto the key, he stepped closer to Father Cecil and placed the locket and medal in his hand.

Father Cecil felt them carefully.

"Ah," he smiled. "Christopher." His smile faded as his fingers felt the back of the medal. "What's this?" he asked turning the medal over.

"It's an engraving," Charlie answered. "But it doesn't make sense. I think it's the address of the original owner or something."

"What does it say?"

"It says, '1 8 9 6 N W 1 0 S T—' The rest of it seems to be worn off."

Father Cecil sat back sharply in his chair.

"What's wrong?"

"You said your grandmother gave that to you?"

"Yes," Charlie answered, becoming very concerned. "Why? What's it mean?"

"Nothing," Father Cecil said, and shook his head. "Charlie, what you are feeling is normal. As you mentioned, Stephen was not much older than you. Death will eventually claim us all, no matter what our age. I was just reading this," he said, picking up his Bible. He felt the top of the page and flipped them rapidly, then stopped. "Here it is. It's in the book of Ecclesiastes. Solomon said, 'Time and unforeseen occurrences befall them, us, all.' Do you understand what it says?"

"Not really," Charlie answered.

"Simply put, whether it's due to time, age, or something unforeseen, like the car accident, we will all die. It just happens. So, we can't spend our lives worrying about when it may come."

"I see," Charlie said, and nodded.

"Well, I think we should call it a day. You may go for

now."

"But—" Charlie hesitated, looking at the dust rag and around the room.

"It's okay. The best thing for you now is to be with your friends." He smiled and stood up.

Charlie reluctantly headed for the door.

"Oh, before you go," Father Cecil spoke up. "Charlie, don't show that medal to anyone else. Keep it safely hidden."

Charlie protectively put his hand over the medal and key then tucked his treasures back under his cassock. "Okay, I will. I mean, I won't. I mean, I won't show anyone and I'll keep it hidden. But can I ask you why?"

"Charlie, it's not an address, it's a map," Father Cecil told him.

"A map?" Charlie repeated, putting his hand instantly to his chest and feeling the medal beneath his robes.

"Remember, not a word to anyone," Father Cecil warned. "Now, run along."

"Yes, Father."

Once in the hallway, Charlie quickly headed for the place where he knew Howard would be, in the bell tower. As he started up the wooden stairs, he stayed close to the wall. Lately the stairs seemed to be shaking more than usual. About halfway up, he froze and balanced himself until the stairs stopped moving. Cautiously he made it to the top.

The afternoon sun was bright. Charlie squinted when he emerged into the belfry. He spotted Howard on the other side of the large bells, looking out the north window.

"Hey, where'd you get those?" he asked when he saw the binoculars in Howard's hands.

"Brother Gregory," Howard answered and continued looking into the distance. "He didn't want them anymore and said I could have them."

"For keeps?"

"Yep."

"What are you looking at?"

"I'm watching Kenneth. He's talking with some guy by a black Cadillac. Man, one of these days I'm gonna get me one of those."

"What are they doing?"

Howard gave Charlie an are-you-nuts look, and returned to looking through his binoculars. "How should I know? These help you see, not hear. But the guy doesn't appear to be happy."

Charlie looked at the garage in the distance, but from where he stood, his view was not as clear as Howard's.

He could see the garage, but the cars all looked the same to him. Suddenly, a black car turned around and sped away.

"Was that him?" he asked.

"Yep."

"So, what's Kenneth doing now?"

"He's heading inside the garage, probably going to the tunnel."

Howard put the binoculars down and walked over to the east window.

"So, how was your morning with Father Cecil?"

"It was okay," Charlie answered, playing it cool. He was still debating whether or not to tell Howard about the medal. He walked across the belfry to the south window and looked out. Over the tops of the tall trees, he could see the valley and the farmlands in the distance. Their varied shades of green and golden yellow looked like the quilt his grandmother made him, which his Uncle Chester promptly took away and gave to one of his boys. He wished he could talk to her now, tell her about the medal. Did she know it's a map? Is that what she wouldn't tell me? Why? Then he remembered the last time he telephoned her, his Uncle Chester had answered and sternly told him not to call again. Should I risk it? He silently wondered.

"Charlie!" Howard said in a harsh whisper, jolting him out of his thoughts.

"What?"

"Look at that!" Howard said, pointing down at two boys by Our Lady of the Subway.

Charlie looked to where Howard was pointing. He recognized the two immediately. It was Gus and Kenneth. Gus was holding out his hand to Kenneth. Kenneth looked around before he pulled a small box from the pocket of his robes and gave it to Gus.

"I knew that's where Gus was getting them! Just you wait 'til I get my hands on that creep," Howard growled as they watched Gus and Kenneth part ways.

"We can deal with that later," Charlie said, pulling the chain from beneath his collar. "Father Cecil told me not to say anything but I have to tell someone. You're my best friend and I trust you, so I'll tell you. I've got *big* news."

Howard turned toward Charlie. "What's more important that saving our friend from that jerk?"

"This," Charlie answered, showing Howard the backside of the medal.

Howard glanced at it and frowned. "I've seen that already. We don't know what it means, so big woo."

"It's a map!" Charlie blurted.

"What? Says who?"

"Says Father Cecil."

"How does he know? He's blind, Charlie."

"Blind but not deaf and dumb," Charlie snapped back.

"He said—told me, it's not an address. It's a map."

Howard took the medal from Charlie's hand and pulled it closer to him, pulling Charlie along with it. He squinted and looked at the etching.

"So, 1 8 9 6 is what?"

"I don't know yet."

"N W stands for northwest?"

"Possibly," Charlie shrugged.

"1 0 S T means…?" Howard asked.

"I don't know that either."

Howard released the medal, freeing Charlie.

"So, all we need to do is figure out what the 1 8 9 6 means, find it, and maybe it will tell us what 1 0 S T is and how northwest figures into it?" Howard said sarcastically.

"I don't have all the answers yet," Charlie said turning away from Howard and toward the window overlooking Black Butte. "I just have this feeling that the answer is out there."

"Oh, for crying out loud," Howard snapped. "Will you give it a rest?"

"Hey, look at that!" shouted Charlie, suddenly pointing toward the valley beyond the butte. "There's smoke coming from that field over there."

Howard turned and looked out at the farmland. "I guess they started a bit early this year."

"What?"

"Some of the farmers burn their fields every few years after harvesting their crops. They call it field burning. They say it sterilizes the ground or something. Sometimes, when the wind blows this way, we can smell the smoke up here for days. It's nothing."

"Oh." Charlie nodded.

"Come on, let's get out of here," Howard said, and

headed for the stairs.

SMOKE

"Good morning, boys," Father Blaise greeted from his usual place at the head of the table in the candle studio. "Are you all ready to get started on our next candle project?"

None of the boys answered. They just looked at each other with an indifferent expression, which did not seem to bother the old priest. He walked over to his desk and began rummaging through the heap of books and papers on it.

"In way of review, this summer you have learned how to make rolled candles, stacked candles, use sand to make a mold, use metal and rubber molds—" Father Blaise stopped in mid-sentence, his eyes darting from side to side, not focusing on anything, his mouth continuing to form words unspoken.

Charlie grabbed Howard's arm and nodded in Father Blaise's direction.

"What?" Howard whispered and looked. When Howard noticed the priest's strange behavior, he stood up. "Father, are you okay?"

Father Blaise stopped moving his lips and looked at Howard. "Yes, dear boy, I'm fine. Why do you ask?"

Howard sat down, shaking his head. "Oh, it's nothing." He looked at Charlie and shrugged.

"Found it!" Father Blaise announced, pulling out a thick, tattered book from the center of the heap and holding it triumphantly in the air. He returned to the head of the work table. "Oh, before we begin, I have a special treat for you. I've sorted through the last batch of candles each of you made and, in your boxes, you'll find your best one. It is yours to do with as you please. They make a wonderful gift. In fact, last year all of my boys donated their candles to be sold at our Oktoberfest booth."

Travis raised his hand immediately.

Father Blaise looked over the top of his book at him. "Yes, Master Bleckinger?"

Travis stood up. "I'd like to donate my candle," he announced with a pious smirk.

"Why, that's very thoughtful of you. Please sit down," Father Blaise said, not so thrilled by Travis's unselfish performance.

Charlie looked at Howard and rolled his eyes.

"For our final candle project this year we will be making the dipped taper candle. For this candle we will be using our tallest, narrow pot called a dipping pot. You will need one pound of wax, cut into small pieces. Why is that, Master Kugele?"

Gus jumped and looked up from his notepad. "Ah, so it will melt quicker?"

"That is correct!" Father Blaise shouted and smiled. "Because dipping pots can't withstand direct heat, you will need to place them in a pot of water to create a sort of double boiler. Remember, I've said this all summer. It is a fire hazard to place any melting pot on direct heat.

"Once your wax is completely melted and reaches 160 degrees, be sure to turn your heat down but keep your water hot enough to maintain your temperature. At his point you want to add five tablespoons of Stearic Acid, your color and scent. Be sure to use your wooden spoons to stir the wax until the color and scent are well blended. If you are using color you will want to stir your melted wax often so the color will not settle to the bottom.

"Once you have finished with that step, the next stage is dipping. I want each of you to cut off a fifteen-inch piece of wick. Tie one end of it to the center of the wooden dowel. On the other end you will want to tie a washer. This will help keep your wick straight. You will hold onto the dowel as you dip your candle.

"We'll stop here and get started," Father Blaise instructed.

"So, what color are you going to make, Gus?" Charlie asked while the two gathered up chunks of wax from the slab Father Blaise was chipping into pieces.

"I don't know," Gus answered indifferently. As he bent down to pick up a sizable chunk of wax, an opened pack of cigarettes fell from his pocket. He quickly grabbed it and shoved it into the pocket of his cassock. He looked at Father Blaise to be sure he had not seen them. Glancing at Charlie, who was looking at him with a frown, he tightened his jaw. "What?" he said defiantly, and headed back to the table.

"I wasn't gonna say a word," Charlie said, following him. Lowering his voice to a whisper, "But since you brought it up, you know you could be in a lot of trouble if you get caught with those, not to mention what you are doing is not good for you."

"And I care because? Oh, let me answer that," Gus said in a mocking tone, "because I'm shortening my life? Because I'm hurting not only myself but my family? Look around, Charlie, I don't have a family. Mind your own business."

"But you have friends, Gus. Friends who care about you and love you *like* family."

"Save it for someone who cares," Gus snapped, and left to fill up his water pitcher in the sink by the door.

"That went well," Howard leaned over and whispered sarcastically to Charlie.

Charlie glared at Howard for a moment, not sure how to take his comment.

"Give him time."

"How much time? Summer's nearly over and he hasn't bounced back."

"I know," Howard agreed.

"I think we should say something to Brother Simon."

"Not yet. Let me try one more time to see if I can get through to him."

"What makes you think you can?" Charlie asked. "None of us have been able to reason with him all summer. It's like he's a completely different person."

"I don't know, but I *do* know involving Brother Simon is *not* going to work. I think we need to figure out another way. I wish Prior Emmanuel were here. What a rotten time for him to die."

Charlie didn't say a word. He just dropped another chunk of wax into his melting pot and tried not to think.

"Well, boys, you all seem to be naturals at this," Father Blaise said while he walked around the room inspecting the pots of melting wax. He paused by Kenneth and leaned over the table to inspect his pot of wax. He took in a deep breath of the rose scent and smiled. "Oh, that's very good, Master DeVries. Master Kaufman, what a superb color. I think it will be your best work this summer."

"Way to go, Dale," Howard congratulated.

Dale smiled, slightly embarrassed by the attention.

"You are all doing a wonderful job with your lesson today," Father Blaise addressed the class. "Let me know when your wax reaches 160 degrees. Then we will commence with the dipping."

The rest of the morning passed quickly. Charlie focused on his candles and forgot about his previous run in with Gus. By the end of class, he had successfully dipped twelve candles.

"Tomorrow we will make some more," Father Blaise announced as the boys retrieved their souvenir candles from the shelf.

Charlie picked up his candle and turned around in time to see Gus disappear out the door followed closely by Kenneth. He shook his head and followed with Howard.

"The wind must be blowing our way," Charlie said covering his nose and mouth with the sleeve of his surplice.

"Ah, the wonderful scent of field burning," Howard took in a deep breath and immediately coughed.

The two hurried up the hill to the Abbey. As they cleared the trees, Charlie removed his sleeve from covering his mouth and took a deep breath.

"That's odd," he said, and looked back toward the candle studio.

"What's odd?" Howard asked, looking over his shoulder.

"I don't smell the smoke anymore."

"It's not all that strange. The fire could be out or the wind shifted. You wanna go see what's going on with the new dorm building."

"Nah, you go on. I'll catch up with you after I take Father Cecil for his walk. He wants to walk down to the orchards, past the pig barns."

"Okay, see you later," Howard said as he and Dale parted company with Charlie.

Moments later, Charlie emerged through the front doors of the Abbey with Father Cecil beside him.

"Not too fast," Father Cecil cautioned as he rested his hand lightly on Charlie's shoulder. The two walked down the front steps of the Abbey. The puttering sounds of the lawnmowers echoed under the portico above them. The scent of freshly cut grass filled the air, making it smell clean. Father Cecil took a deep breath. "I love summer," he said with a smile. "Don't you?"

"I guess," Charlie answered.

"I felt that."

"What?"

"Your shoulders shrugged when you said that. So, you don't like summer?"

"It's not that," Charlie answered. "Step down one more step. It's just that this has been a really hard summer. You remember I told you about my friend Gus? How his cousins were going to adopt him but at the last minute changed their minds?"

"I remember."

"Well, he's still not himself. He's been hanging out with that new guy Kenneth in Saint Peter dorm and I don't think he's a good influence on Gus. Gus has been doing some things he shouldn't be doing."

"Like?"

Charlie's body tensed and he was sure Father Cecil felt it.

"That's okay, Charlie, you don't have to tell me and I won't pry any further. Go on, you were saying how this summer has been hard. Still having trouble over Emmanuel and Stephen?"

"Not as much," Charlie admitted. "Mainly, it's just Gus

I'm worried about now. I don't want to see him get into trouble and I think that's where he's headed."

"Then you need to try to redirect him, or get help from someone who can."

"Oh no!" Charlie gasped. "Don't say anything, here he comes now."

Charlie and Father Cecil stopped just outside the cemetery gate. Gus quickly thrust something into the pocket of his cassock before he smoothed out his surplice.

"Hi, Gus," Charlie greeted as Gus approached them on the narrow path.

"Hi," Gus answered less than enthused. "So, this is Father Cecil I take it?"

Father Cecil smiled and held out his hand. "Yes, I'm Father Cecil. How did you know?"

"Oh, the dark sunglasses, the white cane," Gus answered, shaking Father Cecil's hand, giving it a deliberate jerk.

Charlie glared at Gus, who did not seem to care.

"Oh yes, I forgot," Father Cecil smiled. "So, how are you enjoying your summer?"

"It's okay."

Even Charlie's less-than-keen hearing detected the indifference in Gus's tone. He was sure Father Cecil heard it too.

"Looking forward to school beginning in a few weeks?" Father Cecil continued to make small talk.

"If you say so."

"Hey, we were just going for a walk," Charlie spoke up, slightly embarrassed by his friend. "You wanna come with us?"

"No," Gus said, and just then coughed into his hand.

"Sounds bad, you catching a cold?" Father Cecil asked.

"Yeah, maybe it's one of those summer colds. I think I'll

just go inside. See ya' later." Gus did not wait for a reply. He quickly darted off the path and away from Charlie and Father Cecil, heading away from the building.

"Now, I understand why you're upset," Father Cecil said, once the sound of Gus's footsteps disappeared.

"What do mean?" Charlie looked over his shoulder at the monk.

"How long has he been smoking?"

"How did you know?"

"They say when you lose one of your senses, the others become stronger to compensate. I could smell the smoke on his clothes and I could hear it in his cough."

"Oh, you can't tell anyone," Charlie said, panicked. "Gus would be in so much trouble if Brother Simon or Father Mark were to find out."

"Come on, Charlie, surely you don't think they are that naïve? If I can smell it on him, they can too."

"Please, don't say anything. Let Howard and me find a way to get through to him first. If we can get him to stop then no one needs to know."

"How long has this been going on?"

"Since the start of summer, I think."

"And have you talked to him?"

"Yes," Charlie reluctantly admitted.

Father Cecil shook his head. "The monks here at St. Michael's don't look lightly on anything to do with fire, and an upset teenager smoking is right there on the list of potential hazards."

"Please, Father," Charlie pleaded. "Give us another chance, please."

"All right, I won't say a word, for now," Father Cecil relented. "But, Charlie, if he doesn't come around soon, I will have no choice but to say something to Abbot Ambrose."

"Abbot Ambrose?" Charlie repeated in surprise.

"He's my superior. Come; let's continue our walk, shall we?"

"Okay," Charlie answered. The two continued down the path, passing the cemetery.

They walked in silence. Only the sounds of the birds chirping and of the occasional twig snapping beneath their feet was heard. The path ended when it joined the gravel road. Charlie stopped and looked around curiously. The road from the pig barns came up the hill through the trees, then turned toward the Abbey, but there appeared to be another road, overgrown with weeds and briars, that headed toward the south.

"What is it, Charlie?" Father Cecil asked as he stood resting his hand on Charlie's shoulder.

"Nothing. Just something I haven't noticed before."

"What is it?"

"It's an old road, I think."

"Ah, yes," Father Cecil said, nodding his head. "I believe that's the road to Black Butte."

"Have you ever been out there?" Charlie asked as he continued to peer deeper into the brush.

"It's been years but, yes."

"You have? What's out there?"

"Just the ruins of the old abbey building. Our walk is in the other direction, shall we continue?" Father Cecil gave Charlie's shoulder a gentle nudge, ending their conversation.

An hour later, after seeing Father Cecil back to his room, Charlie walked into St. Nicholas Dorm.

Howard stuck his head out from behind his open locker door. "Well, you were sure gone a long time," he said. "You better hurry or you'll be late for lunch."

"We've got a problem," Charlie whispered while he rushed over to Howard. He took Howard by the arm and pushed him back to a quiet corner by their lockers. "Father Cecil knows about Gus's smoking."

"What? How? Did you tell him?" Howard asked, glaring at Charlie.

"I didn't have to. When we were out walking, we ran into Gus. Father Cecil smelled the cigarette smoke on him."

"So what?" Howard shrugged indifferently.

"So, he's gonna tell Abbot Ambrose if we don't get Gus to stop and soon."

Howard's expression changed instantly to a look of worry. He thought for a moment. "That's not going to be easy. He's pretty stubborn these days."

"Duh!" Charlie retorted. "Got any ideas?"

"Let me think about it. Come on, we best get down to lunch."

The two quickly made their way down the stairs. As they reached the second floor, Charlie noticed Kenneth DeVries standing by the closed fire doors, his hands cupped against the glass windows as he peered inside.

"Come away from there, DeVries," Howard ordered.

Kenneth jumped and spun around.

"What are you doing?" Howard asked indignantly.

"Nothing," Kenneth answered, and ignored Howard's tone. "What's down there?"

"The college classrooms and they're off limits to us," Charlie answered.

"Why?"

"Because, if you haven't noticed," Howard answered. "We're not in college."

"Well aren't you a little curious?" Kenneth asked.

"About what? A classroom's a classroom," Howard answered.

"Hey, Kenneth," Charlie said, stepping closer. "I was wondering. I've noticed that you and Gus are hanging out together. Do you know where he's getting his cigarettes?"

"Charlie!" Howard snapped, jabbing Charlie in the ribs with his elbow.

Kenneth sneered, then all expression drained from his face. "No. I haven't a clue."

Without another word, he walked past them and hurried down the stairs.

"Oh, that was brilliant," Howard snapped. "Why don't you just announce it at dinner tonight?"

"Okay, I get it," Charlie said as the two started down the stairs.

"What were you thinking? Now he's gonna tell Dougary and those other morons in St. Paul."

"I was thinking that maybe if Kenneth is the one giving him the cigarettes that we could scare him off. If we dry up Gus's supply then our problem is solved."

"Nice try but now we have even less time and a bigger problem on our hands. If Father Vicar finds out then Gus is as sure as gone."

Charlie stopped as they reached one of the visitation rooms on the first floor that had its door open. He covered his nose.

"Smells like the wind's shifted again," he said pausing for a moment and looking into the room. The room was filled with a smoky haze. The curtain bellowed in the faint breeze. "I think they should keep the windows closed."

"Me too, but come on, we don't have time. You're gonna make us late," Howard said. He grabbed Charlie by the arm and pulled him away.

As they passed another visitation room with its door open, Charlie glanced inside. He noticed the window was open but there was no smoke. He looked over his shoulder toward the first room. then turned back as the refectory doors opened.

"This place is going to burn," he said quietly to himself.

FIRE

Charlie and Howard sat in their cubicle, thumbing through Howard's stack of comic books. They had read all of them several times and were just bored.

"You know, we should make our own comic book," Howard suggested. "I'm sure between the two of us we could do it. We've sure read enough of them."

"The only problem is that neither of us knows how to draw worth beans," Charlie said. He looked up and cocked his head to one side listening. "Do you hear that?"

"What?" Howard asked, and turned his head to listen. The noise in the hallway grew louder. He quickly closed his comic book and sat up on his bed. "He's back!"

Just then the dormitory doors opened, and a group of boys walked in carrying their suitcases. Charlie jumped to his feet and quickly spotted Rick Walters.

"Great! Just shoot me now," Howard groaned. He fell back on his bed and covered his face with his comic book.

"What are you doing here?" Rick shouted in surprise, seeing Gus sitting in the lounge.

"Oh no!" Charlie gasped and rushed to the lounge. Howard threw his magazine aside and followed him.

"I live here, what's your excuse?" Gus snapped.

"But I thought you were—"

"Rick!" Charlie interrupted. "Great to see you!" He threw his arms around Rick and gave him a hug. "How was your summer?" he asked, backing him away from the lounge.

"MacCready, let me go, you Quimby," Rick said and squirmed free. "What's going on?"

"We'll tell you, you dolt, just keep your voice down," Howard answered. He took Rick's suitcase and pushed him in the direction of the cubicle in the opposite corner of the dorm from his and Charlie's. "We'll help you unpack."

"What's Gus still doing here?"

"We'll explain, just lower your voice and keep moving," Howard whispered.

"I'm out of here!" Gus announced. He slammed his book closed and threw it in the direction of his bed. He stormed out of the dorm in a huff, slamming the doors against the wall.

Howard threw Rick's suitcase onto the bed. "Way to go, Walters."

"What?" Rick looked at them, confused. "What did I do?"

"What did I do?" Howard mocked, and shoved Rick. Rick stumbled backward, sitting on his bed, looking at them both confused.

"'What are you doing here?' Could you be any more lame?" Howard sneered.

"Why's that lame?" Rick asked, starting to get mad but staying seated on the edge of his bed. "I thought Gus got adopted? Why's he still here?"

"Well, obviously it didn't work out," Howard answered.

"Oh no!" Rick gasped. His angered expression changed to

sincere concern. "I had no idea. When I left, I didn't see him on the front steps and figured his cousins had picked him up."

"Well, you figured wrong," Howard snapped back.

Charlie gave Howard a stern look. "Fair enough," he said calmly, turning back to Rick. "Gus must have already been in the bell tower. Honest mistake."

"It was a mistake," Howard said. "The jury's still out on the honest part."

Ignoring Howard's jab, Rick looked at Charlie. "So, how is he?"

"Not good." Charlie looked over his shoulder in the direction of Gus's cubicle.

"Well, have you talked to Prior Emmanuel?"

Charlie and Howard looked at each other as if stunned.

"What? What did I say now?" Rick asked.

Howard looked at the floor. Charlie sat down next to Rick. Quietly, slowly he explained the events of summer. Rick sat in stunned silence as he listened.

"And Stephen too?" he said in disbelief.

"Yeah," Charlie answered.

"I had no idea." Rick's voice quivered as he tried to make sense of what he had been told.

"That's not the half of it," Howard said. Just then the dinner bell rang out. "Oh crap!"

"Howard!" Charlie snapped.

"We're late!" Howard said and headed for the door.

"We'll finish this later," Charlie said and quickly followed.

Minutes later Rick was seated in his usual spot next to Gus at the Saint Nicholas table in the refectory. He looked around for Charlie and Howard but did not see them anywhere. He leaned over and whispered to Gus.

"Where are they?"

Gus just turned and glared at Rick.

Abbot Ambrose walked around to the front of the head table and stood with his hands clasped in front of him. His blue eyes twinkled behind his spectacles while he smiled at everyone.

"Welcome to Saint Michael's," he greeted and opened his arms wide. "My name is Abbot Ambrose. I am the head of Saint Michael's Abbey. Father Mark is your Dean. He is over the four Prefects, Brother Simon for Saint Nicholas Dormitory, Brother Conrad for Saint Thomas, Brother Owen for Saint Sebastian and Father Vicar for Saint Peter Dormitory.

"For some of you, you are returning for another year of instruction. For others, this is your first year with us. Be assured all of us will do our best to make you feel at home."

Charlie stood in the kitchen listening to his great-uncle, unaware of the whispers going on beside him.

Ted Wilson, from Saint Peter, gave Charlie a nudge.

"What?" Charlie turned to him and whispered.

"I said, did you hear about the fire?"

Charlie looked at his former dorm-mate confused. The fire in the candle studio had been a week ago. "What fire?"

"Someone lit a fire down by the pig barns. If it hadn't been for one of the brothers coming to feed the pigs, the whole barn would have gone up in flames."

Charlie's eyes widened. "When did this happen?"

"It was a couple weeks ago. The brothers are keeping it hushed up. They don't want to alarm us, I guess."

A chill ran up Charlie's spine as he remembered smelling smoke when he left the candle studio. He thought it was field burning but maybe.... Suddenly he remembered the visitation room. He turned to Howard standing next to him.

"Hey, cover for me," he whispered.

"Why, where are you going?"

Charlie rolled his eyes and bobbed his head.

"Oh," Howard said. "Don't be too long. Next time, go before dinner."

"Thanks."

Charlie put his tray down and slipped out the kitchen door into the hall. When he passed by the refectory doors, he heard Father Mark talking. He quickly made his way to the main hall. He glanced into the first visitation room and saw everything was normal. The sound of applause filled the hall. Charlie knew he had to hurry. He half-ran to the room where he had seen and smelled the smoke.

Cautiously he entered the room, looking around. Everything appeared normal. A large bouquet of freshly cut roses in a crystal vase sat on the sideboard filling the air with its scent. The loveseat and two wingback chairs were in the center around a coffee table. Charlie walked to the center of the room. He turned around and froze.

"Master MacCready, shouldn't you be in the refectory?"

"Yes, Brother Owen."

Brother Owen walked into the room and looked around suspiciously. "Just what are you doing in here?"

"Nothing," Charlie answered a bit too quickly.

Brother Owen raised an eyebrow and eyed Charlie intently. "I suggest you get back to your duties in the refectory immediately. I will talk with Abbot Ambrose to see what we will do about this situation."

"Yes, Brother."

Charlie quickly slipped past the thin monk and into the hall. Figuring he was already in big trouble he ran back to the kitchen.

Howard and the other waiters had finished serving their tables and were seated. Charlie slowly entered the refectory through the side door by the head table. He could feel the prefects and Abbot Ambrose looking at him but he did not look back. He slipped into his chair next to Howard.

"What took you so long?" Howard asked.

"I got caught," Charlie admitted, and frowned.

Howard gave him a curious look.

"I'll tell you later, in the tower."

"So, what's with you guys?" Rick asked, looking at the two of them.

"What do you mean?" Charlie asked nervously.

"What happened to the brothers?"

"Oh," Charlie said and relaxed.

"Father Mark decided last summer that the members of each dorm will wait on their own table. The brothers aren't going to wait on us anymore," Howard answered.

"Starting Sunday, we're going to be assigned a week at a time," Charlie added.

"Not me," Rick said shaking his head.

"Wanna bet?" Howard smirked.

After dinner, Howard, Charlie, and Rick met in the tower. The sun was still shining high above the tops of the distant mountains. They would have a couple more hours before sunset.

"So, do I want to know what you were doing when you said you got caught in the bathroom?" Howard asked.

"I didn't go to the bathroom," Charlie admitted. "You remember a couple weeks ago when we were leaving the candle studio, we smelled smoke? I thought it was field burning."

"Vaguely," Howard answered.

"Well, Ted just told me that someone tried to burn down the pig barns. The brothers are trying to keep it hushed up because they don't want to frighten us."

"Wha—" Howard breathed his eyes wide in surprise.

"How did he find out?"

"Beats me," Charlie shrugged.

"So, what's that got to do with you not going to the bathroom?" Rick asked even more confused.

"Last week, on our way to dinner, when we passed one of the visiting rooms, I smelled smoke. At the time I didn't think anything of it because the windows were open and I figured it was just field burning. But when we passed another one, I noticed that the windows were open and there was no smoke. I had an awful feeling inside me that this place was going to burn."

"Did you tell anyone?" Rick asked, stepping away from the archway and closer to the two.

"No." Charlie answered. "It was just a feeling. Then when Ted told me about the pig barns I had to go back and take a look at the room."

"What did you see?" Rick asked.

"Nothing. It all looked normal. I didn't even smell any smoke, just roses."

"That's when you got caught?" Howard nodded.

"Yeah, Brother Owen caught me," Charlie admitted. "He's going to talk with Abbot Ambrose."

"Do you think we should tell Abbot Ambrose about your suspicions?" Rick asked.

"No!" both boys said at the same time.

Rick recoiled and eyed at them curiously. "Why not? What's going on?"

Again, the boys exchanged looks.

"Alright!" Rick snapped, sounding exasperated. "Out with it."

"We think it might be Gus," Charlie said quietly.

"What? You're nuts," Rick shouted.

"Will you keep your voice down!" Howard snapped.

"Why do you think it was Gus?"

"Because Charlie caught him smoking," Howard answered.

"Smoking? Where did he get—I don't understand."

"That's not surprising," Howard scoffed.

"Gus hasn't been himself all summer, since his adoption fell through, and Howard and I think Gus may be striking out."

"No way," Rick protested shaking his head.

"There've been other incidences too. At the beginning of summer, Ted Wilson got in trouble because someone burned his surplice," Howard continued.

"And there was another fire started in the forest behind the candle making studio. I found one of Gus's ribbons he used to tie around his candles nearby."

Rick looked at them with a puzzled expression. "So, you think Gus is behind it? I don't believe it. What about him smoking? Where is he getting them?"

"He's getting them from the new kid, DeVries," Howard answered, and turned back toward the east arch. He looked down at the grounds below while Charlie continued explaining about Father Cecil smelling smoke on Gus.

"Wow!" Rick sighed. "I think we should tell Brother Simon."

"No!" Howard snapped and spun around so quickly Rick took a step back. "We can't tell anyone until we have a chance to get through to Gus."

"But this has gone too far," Rick protested.

"If Brother Simon or Father Mark find out about Gus then they'll send him away to juvie," Howard said. "That is *not* an option."

Rick looked at Charlie.

"So, what do we do now?"
"I don't know," Charlie answered.

SIRENS IN THE NIGHT

Sleep seemed to elude Charlie. He lay on his back wide-awake staring at the ceiling. The sounds of Howard's snoring and the other boys' breathing tried to lull him to slumber, but Charlie's thoughts resisted. He sat up in his bed and stared out the window.

A blanket of stars covered the clear sky above. The glow from the half-moon cast long shadows of the trees across the Great Lawn. Charlie turned and looked at the new building. The lights by the entrance were lit but the rest of the building was dark. The feeling that none of them would be moving into it as planned flashed in his mind.

A rustling from the cubicle on the other side of the partition beside Howard's bed pulled Charlie's attention away from the outside. Slowly he crawled to the foot of his bed, to see what was going on. In the dim light that shone through the windows, he could only see a shadowy figure make its way out of the dorm. He knew it was Gus.

Charlie crawled back under his covers. He closed his eyes and pushed all thoughts of Gus and his problems out of his mind.

In the morning the new school year would begin, the start of his sophomore year. He heard the sophomores from last year complaining about how hard the classes were and he wondered if he could do it. At last sleep found Charlie.

Suddenly the silence of the night was shattered by the blaring siren in the hall. The lights came on. Charlie and Howard jumped out of their beds at the same time and crashed into each other. They both fell back onto their beds, dazed and confused.

"What's going on?" Charlie asked, rubbing his forehead.

Howard grabbed his glasses and rushed to the center lounge. Charlie quickly grabbed his robe and followed.

"What is that?"

"What's happening?" groaned some of the older boys, turning over and putting their pillows over their heads. Some of the younger boys, frightened by the noise, huddled around Howard and Charlie in the lounge.

The dormitory doors flew open. Brother Simon, dressed in his long black bathrobe over his white nightshirt, rushed to the center of the dorm.

"Silence!" his voice thundered over the loud wail of the siren.

The boys still in their beds jumped to their feet at the sound of his voice.

"I want you to calmly put on your robes and slippers and line up, single file."

The boys quickly did as they were told and lined up in the center of the dorm. One of the younger boys standing beside Howard whimpered. Brother Simon stopped in front of him.

"Master Fletcher, stop crying," he ordered.

"But it's so loud," Timmy said, his hands over his ears.

"I know, but everything will be okay," Brother Simon

reassured him in a gentle understanding tone. "Master Miller, will you...."

"Yes, Brother," Howard answered and put his arm protectively around Timmy's shoulders.

Brother Simon walked down the line. He paused when he came to the place where Gus should have been standing. A concerned look came over his face. He spun around to see Gus's empty cubicle. Turning back to the boys, his stern expression returned.

"Does anyone know where Master Kugele has gone?"

"I saw him leave the dorm after lights out but I'm not sure how long ago," Charlie spoke up.

Brother Simon eyed Charlie angrily, yet deep in thought.

"Master Thurman, I want you to lead the boys in a single file down the hall to the east stairwell. Father Mark is waiting there, and will instruct you further. Is that clear?"

"Yes, Brother Simon," Bobby Thurman, a senior student, answered. He took his place at the front of the line and they all began to file out of the dormitory.

When Charlie passed by Brother Simon, he glanced up at him. Brother Simon stood, back rigidly straight and tall, shoulders back, hands tucked into the sleeves of his black robe. He turned and followed Charlie out of the dorm.

As they entered the hallway, the line stopped.

"What's going on?" Gus asked looking at everyone.

"Master Kugele," Brother Simon yelled above the noise of the siren. "Get in line. We will talk later."

Gus did as he was told, and slipped behind Howard. The line continued to move.

Bobby turned away from the nearest stairwell and headed toward the one by Saint Peter dorm. Charlie glanced back over his shoulder just in time to see two monks emerge from the monastery wing. They paused briefly, and spoke to Brother Simon. Brother Simon pointed toward St. Nicholas's dormitory and the monks hurried inside. Charlie stopped to watch. Moments later the two monks reappeared carrying the trunk from the lounge. They quickly went through the double doors, back into the monastery wing, the doors closing behind them.

"Master MacCready!"

Charlie jumped and turned around. The line of his dorm mates was gone. Only Father Mark stood at the top of the stairs.

"Hurry up! Don't dawdle!" he snapped.

Charlie hurried over to the stairs.

"Stay to the right," Father Mark instructed as the two started down the stairs.

"What's going on?" Charlie asked.

"Hush and keep walking," Father Mark said. "Don't run."

As they caught up with the others, Charlie could hear some of them saying something about smoke. Suddenly the realization hit him. Fire!

The boys in front of him began to choke and gag, covering their mouths with their hands. Charlie inhaled but smelled nothing. As he reached the second floor where the seminary's classrooms were, he glanced through the windows of the fire doors. A sudden chill ran up his spine as he saw the hallway filled with thick black smoke. He froze, unable to move.

"Keep going, son," Father Mark said, putting his hand on Charlie's shoulder and turning him away from the doors. "Everything will be all right." He gave Charlie a gentle nudge and the two continued down the stairs.

Once outside, the boys gathered in groups by dorm on the Great Lawn. Fire engines, lights flashing, sirens blaring, roared up the drive. Firemen leapt from their trucks and began pulling long hoses from the compartments on the back ends of the trucks. They quickly attached them to a nearby fire hydrant and made their way into the Abbey.

Charlie quickly found Howard and Rick standing amid a small group of boys from their dorm.

"I don't believe this," he whispered to Howard.

Howard did not respond. His eyes were fixed on the red glow behind several windows on the second floor.

Charlie looked over his shoulder. Behind him, across the front lawn, the boys had left their dorm lines and gathered in clusters. Older ones were comforting some of the younger, frightened boys while keeping an eye on the Abbey.

Toward the edge of the lawn, at the front of the fire trucks, Charlie spotted Gus, alone. He did not know why he had not noticed it before, but Gus wasn't in his bathrobe. He was not even wearing pajamas. Instead he was dressed in jeans and a coat.

Suddenly there was an explosion and the sound of glass shattering. Charlie jumped back and looked at the building. Flames shattered the window and shot up the side of the building, reaching the fourth floor. Charlie froze. He recognized the window on the fourth floor. It was his window.

The firemen quickly aimed their hoses at the broken window. The flames retreated for a moment and then another window on the second floor shattered sending more flames up the side of the building.

Charlie looked toward the monastery wing. Abbot Ambrose approached Father Mark, Brother Simon, Father Vicar, and the other dormitory heads. As he spoke to them, he motioned toward the boys and then toward the new building. Everyone nodded and then dispersed. Charlie watched as Brother Simon seemed to walk directly toward Howard, Rick and him.

"The boys from St. Nicholas's dorm," Brother Simon called across the front lawn, "line up!"

Similar calls rang out over the drone of the fire trucks' engines, and once again the boys lined up according to their dorms.

While Gus took his place in line, Charlie gave Howard a nudge getting his attention. He nodded in Gus's direction. Howard leaned forward and looked at Gus. He looked at Charlie and shrugged as though saying, "What?"

"Master MacCready!" Brother Simon snapped.

Charlie jumped and looked straight ahead.

Brother Simon gave him a disapproving look.

"Abbot Ambrose wants us to clear the Great Lawn. He has opened the new Hall and we can all wait inside the auditorium. Master Thurman, you may lead the way."

"Yes, Brother Simon," Bobby answered.

The boys walked single file across the lawn to the new building. Though Charlie was still thinking about Gus, he was excited to see the inside of the new residence hall again.

The foyer was large and felt cold to Charlie. The recessed lights in the ceiling filled the room with a dim glow. The sound of their footsteps on the polished brick floor echoed in the empty room. Obediently the boys followed Bobby over to the large oak doors in the north wall. The doors blended so perfectly with the wood panels on the wall Charlie did not see them at first.

As he stepped into the back of the auditorium and looked around, Charlie thought the room looked a little larger than their refectory in the Abbey. In the opposite corner from the entrance doors was a small raised platform. A series of horizontal wooden slats formed a canopy above the stage and created a flat backdrop as it met the floor. A podium stood center stage. Two cushioned chairs sat behind it at opposite ends of the stage. The lights in the windowless auditorium were dimmed.

Charlie slid into the seat next to Howard. "Did you see him?"

"See who?" Howard said.

"I wanted you to look at Gus."

"Yeah, I did. So?"

Charlie shook his head. He looked around the auditorium for their friend. Gus was sitting off by himself. His arms were folded over his chest in a self-hug sort of way. His eyes were fixed in a cold stare at something or someone across the room. His knee was bouncing as though he was about to pounce.

"Look at what he's wearing," Charlie told Howard.

Howard leaned forward and looked across the room at Gus. "So, he's wearing his coat and jeans." As he sat back, his eyes widened and he quickly sat forward again, taking another look.

"You see what I mean."

"Yeah," Howard agreed.

"I couldn't sleep, so I was just lying there looking out the window when I heard him get up. I thought he was just going to the restroom, so I didn't think anything of it. But, since when do you get dressed to go to the can?"

"Something's up," Howard said. "And I think we should find out before Brother Simon gets to him first."

"Agreed."

The boys stood up and made their way over to the empty chairs beside Gus. Howard sat down on one side of him and Charlie the other.

Gus's knee stopped fidgeting for a moment. He glanced at them, then returned to looking across the auditorium. "What?" he demanded more than asked.

"That's what we want to know," Howard said. "Charlie saw you leave the dorm just before the sirens started."

Gus turned sharply and looked at Charlie. "So, you're still spying on me?"

"No. I just happened to be awake when you got up, that's all."

"So, aren't you a little overdressed to go to the john?" Howard asked.

"Yeah, if I was going to the john," Gus answered.

Howard and Charlie looked at each other, their eyes wide and their mouths agape.

"So, you weren't headed to the bathroom?" Charlie lowered his voice to a whisper.

"No," Gus said shaking his head.

"Then where were you going?" Howard asked.

Gus looked at him sharply. "That's for me to know and you to find out." He stood up and pushed past Charlie, walking to the other side of the auditorium.

Charlie watched Gus settle into a chair away from everyone else. Gus wrapped his arms around himself and resumed his blank stare. Charlie's mind was a flurry of conflicting thoughts. He turned back toward Howard.

"Are you thinking what I'm thinking?"

Howard furrowed his brow and looked confused. "Depends. What are you thinking?"

"I'm thinking this is too big for us to handle. We need to tell Brother Simon or someone."

"No!" Howard snapped in a harsh whisper. "We can't do that."

"What if he hurts someone?"

"We don't really know he started this fire. We've got no proof," Howard said. "Let's wait until we find out more."

Charlie sat back in his seat. "Okay," he agreed. He slid down in his chair and yawned. The next thing he knew, the room was flooded with light and the noise from all of the boys talking at once.

"Okay, quiet down," Father Mark said, standing on the raised platform at the front of the auditorium. He held his outstretched arms over their heads and slowly lowered them. As he did, the boys became silent.

Charlie looked around the room and noticed Brother Simon standing with the other prefects in the back. Father Vicar stood at one end of the four and Brother Simon at the other, their backs straight, hands hidden beneath their robes, faces stony and expressionless like two gargoyles. Charlie turned back around.

"The fire is out," Father Mark announced. The room instantly filled with cheers and applause. Again, Father Mark's arms went up, silencing them. "The fire was contained to one classroom on the second floor, although the smoke has affected all of the rooms to a degree."

"Do they know what caused it?" a voice from the middle of the auditorium called out.

Father Mark looked confused as his eyes searched for the person who had asked the question. Giving up, he shook his head. "Not yet. But this is an old building and there could be several possible causes. The fire department will be investigating.

"Now, your dorm prefects and I have made a thorough inspection of the fourth floor. You'll be happy to know that it is clear. The fire doors did their job and there is only a faint trace of smoke in the air. So, you may all return to your dorms.

"Due to the events of the night, there will be no classes today. Instead, silence will be observed on the fourth floor the entire day. Those of you who wish to get some rest can. We are also adjusting mealtime this morning. We will have a brunch in the refectory at ten-thirty, then a snack will be brought to your dorms at three. The servers will not be needed this morning."

"That's good," Charlie leaned closer to Howard and whispered.

"Amen to that," Howard agreed.

"And one last thing," Father Mark continued. "Please be careful on the stairs and use the handrails. There may still be some water. That is all. You may all quietly return to your dorms."

When Charlie followed Howard into St. Nicholas dorm, he took a deep breath. Father Mark was right; there was only a faint lingering smell of smoke. He walked through the lounge, passed the trunk, straight to his cubicle. He flopped down on his bed and turned away from the soot-blackened window. All he could think about was sleep.

A PYROMANIAC IN OUR MIDST

Charlie had no idea what to expect as he lined up with the other boys at ten-thirty outside the refectory doors. He could not smell a thing after passing the second floor and getting a whiff of the lingering wet smoke. He had no idea what a brunch was. Still, he knew he was hungry, and anything sounded good.

When the doors of the refectory opened, the boys began to file in but were immediately stopped. Father Vicar stood with his hands raised. As soon as he was sure he had their full attention, he lowered his hands and hid them in the folds of his habit. Holding his head back, he looked down his nose at the boys in front of him and said, "This morning we will be dining cafeteria-style."

Charlie gave the back of Howard's head a curious look. "Cafeteria-style?" he whispered confused.

"One by one," Father Vicar continued, "you will pick up a tray and silverware, then move down the line. The brothers will dish up your plate, then hand it to you. You will then take it to your table and stand until all have been served. We will then have a prayer and eat in silence."

"Silence?" some of the boys groaned.

"Silence!" Father Vicar echoed loudly. He then nodded, and the line proceeded to move slowly.

To Charlie's surprise, brunch looked a lot like breakfast. There were sweet rolls, scrambled eggs with chopped up ham, hash brown potatoes, pancakes, sausages, bacon, and fresh fruit. Charlie asked for a little of everything.

While he stood waiting for the other boys to finish being served, Charlie looked around the refectory to see what the other boys had on their trays. When he looked at Gus's tray, he was surprised to see it was practically empty. There was a small portion of eggs and a slice of toast on his plate. Charlie looked up to see Gus glaring back at him. Charlie smiled and looked away.

As the boys ate, Father Vicar paced the rows, making sure that no one broke the rule of silence. Charlie was about to whisper to Howard when a faint voice was heard over at St. Sebastian's table. Father Vicar was swift in silencing it and pronouncing judgment against the offender, two hours of work crew.

After the meal, Father Vicar walked to the head table and clapped the wooden block against it. All eyes turned toward him.

"This afternoon silence will continue to be observed not only in the dormitories but the entire fourth floor as well," Father Vicar instructed. "You are free to move about the hilltop but stay away from the second floor and out of the way of the investigators.

"The Altar Boys need to check in with their assignments and spend some time with them immediately following dismissal."

Charlie's shoulders slumped. He sighed and frowned at

Howard and Rick. They would have to wait to get together until after they had seen their brothers.

"Let us pray," Father Vicar said and looking heavenward, stretched out his arms. Charlie and the rest of the boys bowed their heads.

After the prayer, the boys were dismissed. Quietly they made their way into the hall. At least on the first floor they were free to talk but most of the boys continued to do so in a whisper, fearing the wrath of Father Vicar in case they were breaking one of his unspoken rules.

Charlie, Howard and Rick slipped away from the rest of the boys and headed for the monastery wing. As they neared Abbot Ambrose's office, they could hear loud voices inside and slowed so they could eavesdrop.

"I don't believe it," Abbot Ambrose was heard saying.

"That is what our preliminary findings are, Father Abbot. The fire started in a wastebasket that was placed under the wooden desk next to the bookcase and windows. There's no other explanation, the fire was deliberately set," said a voice the boys did not recognize.

"Abbot Ambrose," Brother Conrad spoke next. "Do you think that the fire in the visiting room and this one could be connected?"

"What fire? You had another fire and didn't notify us?" the unrecognized voice said sounding angry.

"It wasn't a big deal," Abbot Ambrose explained. "It burned itself out before we even knew about it. There was no real damage, just a lot of smoke. We cleaned it up. You don't think they could be related, do you?"

"We have no way of knowing for sure now. However, there is a strong possibility—"

"You can't possibly mean we have an arsonist in our

midst?" Brother Owen interrupted.

"No! It's unthinkable," Father Mark said firmly. "I don't agree."

"I understand your reluctance, Father. Still, I think it would be unwise to disregard the possibility so quickly. We will continue our investigation. I leave the rest up to you."

"Thank you," Abbot Ambrose said.

"Father Abbot, may I have a word with you?" Brother Owen spoke up again as the knob on the door turned.

Charlie, Howard and Rick quickly slipped out the door of the student wing and into the foyer of the Abbey's main entrance before the men emerged from Abbot Ambrose's office.

Howard pulled them into a corner.

"Bell tower, in an hour," Howard said, leaving no room for a discussion.

Moments later Charlie stood in front of Father Cecil's door. Today he was nervous about seeing his friend. He remembered their walk and Father Cecil's warning that time was running out. Hesitantly he knocked.

From inside he heard a rustling before the door opened. Father Cecil stood staring blankly over Charlie's head.

"Ah, Charlie," he greeted but there wasn't his usual smile. "Come in, we have a lot to talk about."

Charlie's stomach tightened. Suddenly he wished he had not been so greedy at brunch. He walked into the dark room and closed the door behind them.

"You may want to turn on the light," Father Cecil said as he made his way across the room to his chair. "I'm used to the darkness, but I know you aren't."

Charlie flipped the light switch and the light in the center of the ceiling came on.

"Have a seat."

Charlie pulled out the chair by the table and sat down. He watched Father Cecil straighten his habit while he sat in his chair.

"I take it everyone is okay?"

"Yes," Charlie answered. "Are you?"

"No, Charlie, I'm not," came Father Cecil's terse reply. "You have no idea how frightening it is to be awakened by the sound of a siren. When I open my eyes it's still dark. I can't see why or what is causing the alarm like you can. I have to wait for one of my brothers to come to help me out of the building all the while I'm wondering and imagining what is happening.

"Do you know what an accomplice is?"

"Not exactly," Charlie answered.

"It's someone who helps someone else do something bad. I am an accomplice. You are an accomplice. We both kept silent about what we knew. I should have gone to my superior, Abbot Ambrose, and told him after our walk and run in with your young friend. Instead, I kept quiet.

"Charlie, what if someone would have been hurt last night? This has to stop and now."

Charlie looked at the floor. "I know. You're right. I'm sorry. I never thought he would do—"

"So, you think it was your friend's doing?" Father Cecil interrupted.

Charlie did not look up. He just stared at the floor. "Yes, Father," he answered. "Last night I couldn't sleep, and I saw him leave the dorm after lights out. When we were out front on the Great Lawn, I noticed he was wearing his jeans and a coat."

"You need to tell Abbot Ambrose before things get worse, and that would be now."

Charlie looked up sharply, his heart pounding as he thought about having to tell on his friend.

"You should go."

"But—"

"We will talk later," Father Cecil said sternly.

"Yes, Father," Charlie replied.

Just as Charlie entered the hall, Brother Owen walked up. He waited with his arms folded over his chest beneath his robes for Charlie to close the door of Father Cecil's room.

"Master MacCready," he said coldly.

Charlie jumped and turned around. He saw the smug look on Brother Owen's face, a look he was sure meant bad news.

"You think I have forgotten about catching you out of the refectory during dinner last night? Well, think again. Father Abbot and Father Mark want to see you immediately. They are waiting in Father Abbot's office."

The knots in Charlie's stomach tightened more. He looked down the hall, then back at the prefect.

"Yes, Brother Owen," he answered and headed off.

The walk to the Students Wing, to Abbot Ambrose's office, felt like a mile long. He tried to figure out an excuse for not coming forward but everything he came up with sounded lame. He was in trouble and there was no getting out of it. He wished Howard and Rick were with him. Maybe then the punishment would not be so hard, but then again.... He wondered if he would be sent away.

As he stood in front of Abbot Ambrose's door, he took in a deep, unsteady breath and let it out slowly. He had heard doing that would calm one's nerves, but they were wrong. His hand shook as he knocked on the door. It opened so quickly that it startled Charlie.

"Master MacCready," Father Mark greeted in a quiet voice. "We will talk later, come back in two hours." He closed the door.

Charlie stood for a moment and stared at the door, confused, but at the same time, relieved for the temporary reprieve. He turned away and headed for the stairs and the bell tower.

Charlie stood staring out at Black Butte from the south window of the belfry while he waited for Howard and Rick. He was not really thinking about Black Butte. His thoughts were replaying his conversation with Father Cecil. Father Cecil was right. He should have gone to Father Mark about Gus a long time ago. Why did he listen to Howard?

The minutes seemed to pass like hours. Charlie began to pace in front of the giant metal bell. He thought about leaving, waiting for the others down below but then imagined running into Brother Owen in the hall. No, it was better for him to wait in the tower.

Finally, there was a noise from below. Charlie turned around just as Howard popped his head up from below.

"Hey, what are you doing here already?" he asked while he climbed the last couple steps.

Charlie did not say a word. He just stared at Howard in total silence.

"Boy, you look as if you just lost your best friend. Things that bad with Father Cecil?"

Charlie opened his mouth to speak just as Rick climbed into the belfry.

"Hi, guys," he greeted brushing at the dust on his robes. "Hope I didn't keep you waiting long."

"No," Charlie answered. Howard just glared.

"That's good," Rick answered. "So, what're you going to do?"

"We've got trouble," Charlie said. He started to sit down on an old wooden crate they moved into the belfry months earlier but stopped and stood instead.

"What sort of trouble?" Howard asked.

"Father Cecil was really mad today. He blames Gus for the fire and said time's up. He said I made him an accomplice in this and that I need to tell Abbot Ambrose now."

"What!" Howard gasped.

"He's going to tell him himself, so maybe we should come clean."

"No!" Howard snapped back, shaking his head.

"There's more," Charlie admitted. He leaned against the window sill. "Brother Owen told Abbot Ambrose about catching me in the visitation room during dinner last night. He said Father Abbot wants to see me."

"So, did you go?" Rick asked, raising an eyebrow in what appeared to be hopeful anticipation.

"Yes, but Father Mark told me to come back in two hours."

"What?" Howard nearly yelled. "So, you were going to squeal on him?"

"What choice do I have, Howard?"

"You—Charlie, you can't. Gus will get sent away to juvie."

"I wasn't going to tell him that I suspect Gus lit the fire, just that Gus is smoking, and that's all."

Howard thought for a moment.

"What about you getting caught?" Rick asked. "What do you think they're going to say?"

Charlie shook his head. "I don't know. I guess just what I told you guys. What time is it?"

"It's nearly two o'clock," Rick answered.

"Well, I guess I should go."

"Wait," Howard said just as Charlie reached the trap door. "We'll go with you."

"Oh no I won't!" Rick protested.

"Yes, you will," Howard said, grabbing Rick's arm and pulling him over to the hole in the floor. "We're in this together."

"But I had nothing to do with any of this," Rick continued to protest and follow Charlie down the stairs.

"Fine, you can sit outside in the hallway and keep your eyes and ears open," Howard said when they reached the fourth-floor stairwell.

"All right," Rick relented. Reluctantly he followed them down the stairs to Abbot Ambrose's office.

Charlie felt a little braver with Howard standing beside him when he knocked on the door. It opened immediately.

"Come in," Father Mark greeted, eyeing Howard curiously.

"Is it okay if Howard comes in too?"

Abbot Ambrose looked over the top of his spectacles. "Master Miller, I should have known. Come in. Mark, if Master Walters is out there have him come in here too."

Abbot Ambrose rocked back in his chair and rested his elbows on the armrests. He clasped his hands in front of his chest while he waited for the boys to settle into the three chairs beside his oak desk. Father Mark closed the door and sat in the chair across from the Abbot.

Charlie fidgeted in his seat and looked at Howard. Howard appeared calm, but when he glanced at Charlie, the look in his eyes was of uncertainty. Charlie looked at his great-uncle.

"So, Master MacCready," Abbot Ambrose spoke first. "It has come to my attention that you left the refectory last night during dinner. To do what?"

"I went to look at the visitation room next to Father Mark's office."

"Why was that?"

Charlie glanced at Howard again, then looked back at Abbot Ambrose. "When we were headed for dinner, I saw smoke in the room. I thought it was just field burning, but when Ted Wilson told me about the fire in the pig barns, I had to take another look."

"I see," Abbot Ambrose nodded. "What did you expect to find?"

"I don't know."

"Well, I will tell you this, there was a small fire in the room. It burned itself out before doing any real damage. We were lucky that day," Abbot Ambrose explained.

"So, what's your involvement in this, Master Miller?" Father Mark asked.

Howard jumped and shook his head. "Nothing."

Father Mark eyed him suspiciously.

"There is something else," Charlie said, glancing at Howard and Rick, then back at Abbot Ambrose. "Ever since the beginning of summer, I have suspected Gus of smoking. He's been acting very cold to us and not like himself."

"Why didn't you come to Father Mark or me about this sooner?"

"We—I mean I was afraid you'd send Gus away to juvie or something. I thought I could get through to him to stop before anyone found out. Only someone did. I was walking with Father Cecil and we ran into Gus. He smelled smoke on Gus. He was going to tell you himself, but I pleaded with him not to."

Abbot Ambrose looked at Father Mark.

"He's going to talk to you about it today," Charlie added. "Please don't be mad at him. It's not his fault."

"I will deal with Father Cecil," Abbot Ambrose said, and looked back at Charlie. "I must say, while I understand your motive and your loyalty to your friend, I'm disappointed in all three of you for not trusting me or Father Mark enough to come forward sooner."

Howard opened his mouth as if to say something but Abbot Ambrose raised his hand, hushing him. He shook his head. "I will speak with Master Kugele to see if there is any merit to this smoking thing. In the future, I hope you boys will come to us and let us handle the matter should anything arise."

"We will," Howard answered quickly, sounding a bit relieved.

"As for you, Master MacCready," the Abbot continued. "Because you left the refectory during a meal without permission, you will spend two hours this Saturday helping Father Ignatius with a project in the basement."

"Yes, Father Abbot," Charlie acknowledged. He wondered silently what the project was and how long it would take.

"As for the two of you," Abbot Ambrose turned to Rick and Howard. "You will each spend an hour of work crew with Brother Simon this Saturday. That is all."

The three boys stood up and left the office.

A HISTORY LESSON

The basement in the Monastery Wing was quiet and dark, a huge contrast to the basement of the student wing which housed the classrooms. Charlie had never ventured down to this side before, never had a reason to, but today he was to meet Father Ignatius there. A light shone from a doorway at the far end of the hall. Charlie heard humming as he approached the room.

"Father Ignatius?" he called quietly, sticking his head into the room. The room inside was larger than Charlie imagined. A long wall of boxes stacked almost to the ceiling just inside the door hid the room. Cautiously Charlie stepped inside. He looked up and down the aisle. "Father Ignatius, are you in here?"

"Master MacCready, is that you?" a voice called from behind the wall of boxes.

"Yes, Father, it is."

"Well, come on in. I'm over here."

"Okay," Charlie answered. He hurried along the cardboard wall. Turning the corner, he stopped. The wall continued toward the outer basement wall. "Father?" Charlie called as he felt his way along.

"Keep coming," the priest called back.

Charlie reached the end of the wall and stopped. Wary this was a maze and he would get lost forever down inside it, he peeked around the corner. To his relief, there were no more walls. Lighted display cabinets lined the outside wall. Glass display tables were placed helter-skelter among smaller stacks of boxes. Still there was no sign of Father Ignatius.

"Father?" Charlie called making his way around the boxes and tables toward the far side of the room.

"I'm right here," Father Ignatius answered back.

"Oh, there you are." Charlie rounded the corner and let out a scream. He fell backward, crashing into a stack of empty boxes and landing hard on the concrete floor. His eyes were fixed on the menacing black bear standing on its hind legs with its front paws and enormous claws reaching out in front for him. The bear's mouth was open, showing his large sharp teeth but it uttered no sound, not even a growl.

"Master MacCready, are you okay?" Father Ignatius inquired, rushing around another stack of boxes behind Charlie. "Oh, I see you've met Ben. He's really a gentle bear, now that he's dead and stuffed," he continued, helping Charlie to his feet and trying hard to hide his amusement.

"St-stuffed," Charlie repeated, feeling his heartbeat returning to normal and continuing to stare at the still beast. "Why would you have something like that here?"

"It was donated by one of the townspeople, along with a couple of stuffed bobcats and a huge python."

Charlie shuddered. He finally pulled his gaze away from the bear and looked at the priest. Father Ignatius looked just the way Howard had described him, "A short, pot-bellied monk with a W. C. Fields bulbous nose; bald on top but with short grey, almost white hair around his ears and back of his head. If you ask me, he looks like a drinker, if you know what I mean."

Father Abbot's description was kinder. He said that Father Ignatius was the Abbey's historian. Until a few years ago, he was the head librarian, but the job was becoming too much for the eighty-year-old monk. He couldn't keep up with all his duties even with the aid of other brothers. That's when Abbot Ambrose suggested Father Ignatius should retire. After a few months, it became obvious that Father Ignatius was depressed. That's when Abbot Ambrose came up with this new project that would make good use of Father Ignatius's talents, the museum.

"Are you sure you're okay?" Father Ignatius asked.

"I think so, Father," Charlie answered, and nodded. "I can't believe...." He looked at the bear again and began to laugh. Father Ignatius laughed too.

"Well, that was quite the entrance, young Master."

"I'll say," Charlie agreed, and moved away from the bear. "What is all of this?"

"This, my dear boy, is the Abbey's new museum," he announced proudly. "Father Abbot has given me the task of setting up a museum of the Abbey's history. He had all of these boxes brought down from the attic, and now we need to go through them and pull out the things that best reflect the history of our fine Abbey."

"All of these boxes?"

"Oh, don't give me that look," Father Ignatius laughed again. "Trust me, it won't be as daunting as it seems."

"So where do we begin?"

"Over here." Father Ignatius led Charlie around the empty boxes to where he was working in the corner of the museum. "I've started sorting through a few boxes, taking out anything that will help tell the Abbey's story and placing it on the display tables. Everything else I've been repacking into boxes that will be returned to the attic."

"So, what do you want me to do?"

"I think it would go faster if you did the repacking."

"Agreed." Just then, something caught his eye. In an open box was a large, framed, black-and-white photograph of an old one-story building. Charlie gently took it out of the box. "Wasn't this in Prior Anselm's room?" he asked.

"Why yes," Father Ignatius nodded and took the picture from Charlie. "This was the Abbey's very first monastery building."

"Prior Anselm told me it was built on Black Butte."

"That is correct," Father Ignatius nodded. "However, the name the original inhabitants gave this hill was translated Mount of Communion.

"Here, grab yourself one of those boxes and start packing it up." Father Ignatius handed him a pair of old metal bookends.

"So, where did the name Black Butte come from?"

"Legend has it, the native inhabitants called this mountain The Mount of Communion. It was sacred ground to them. They would come here and offer prayers and fire to their gods because it was the highest point in the valley, and closest to their gods in the heavens.

"Then, one fateful year, the natives were stricken with disease, possibly smallpox. The people flocked to this mountain to offer prayers and fire to their gods in order to appease them and ward off the plague. When it finally passed, nearly half of their people had died.

"When the white man eventually showed up, they found the mountain was the ideal location to build their town. Because of its view of the surrounding valley, it provided them protection from possible invaders. The native people, few in number and weak, were unable to put up a fight. The white man ran them off their land, but not before the natives called down a curse on the mountain. Any building that would be constructed on it would see fire.

"Hand me that box over there, please."

Charlie quickly retrieved the box, anxious to learn more.

"The white man ignored the curse. They renamed the hill Lone Butte. On the top of the hill, on the site where the natives worshiped their gods, the white man constructed their walled fortress with a general store and an inn. That first winter was an extremely cold one. Many of the settlers, who had built their houses at the base of the mountain, became sick. They were brought to the inn. That's when tragedy struck. Late one night a fire broke out the ground-floor of the inn. The fire spread quickly from one building to the next with no one able to stop it. The entire fortress burned to the ground in minutes, killing all who were there.

"News of the fire brought back memories of the curse. Some settlers became afraid, packed up what they could, and moved south. Those that stayed were determined to rebuild and they did only to have their buildings burn again.

"After the second fire, the settlers decided to build their town in the valley and abandoned the mountain and its butte."

"Wow," Charlie breathed. "How do you remember all of this stuff?"

Father Ignatius smiled. "I've been here a long time. Speaking of time, looks like we've made a good dent for one day."

"But you haven't told me about the abbey and the butte being called Black Butte," Charlie protested.

"We can continue it another day. Just get permission from Father Abbot."

"I will," Charlie agreed.

"I'll walk you out."

Moments later Charlie was back in the Students Wing heading for Abbot Ambrose's office. He was sure his great-uncle would give him permission to continue helping Father Ignatius. As he turned the corner into the main hall, he saw a policeman enter Abbot Ambrose's office. Curious, he quietly approached and settled in the chair next to the door. He strained his ear to listen.

"Yes, Father, we are positive," the unfamiliar voice said. "It was definitely arson. That means we will want to interview the boys."

"Out of the question," Father Mark snapped. "We won't allow it."

"It's either that or we'll have the state shut you down."

"You wouldn't! Father Abbot?"

"Mark, I'm with the detective on this one. There is just too much at stake here and these are very serious charges."

"So, spying again?"

Charlie jumped and looked up at the stern glare of Brother Owen. "No," he lied. "I'm just waiting to talk with Abbot Ambrose."

"Why don't you do your waiting somewhere else," Brother Owen snarled.

Charlie did not wait to be told again. He jumped to his feet and quickly headed for the tower. He had so much to tell Howard.

THE QUESTIONING

"I can't believe we've been assigned to wait tables again already. What's up with that?" Howard groused while he stood in the doorway between the kitchen and refectory with Charlie.

"It's been six weeks already and waiting on our table isn't *that* bad," Charlie whispered.

"Well, I just hope we don't have to do it on Halloween. It'll mess up my costume plans."

"What are you going as?" Charlie asked, his curiosity piqued.

"I can't tell you or I'd have to kill you," Howard teased.

Charlie laughed, then changed the subject. "So how did it go today?"

"It wasn't so bad," Howard shrugged. "First that detective guy asked me if I minded him recording our conversation. I said, go ahead He asked me to say my name, how old I am and stuff like that."

"Were you nervous?"

"At first, but I figured I don't have anything to hide. So, I just told him what I knew."

"Did you mention Gus?" Charlie leaned closer and whispered.

"No and what's strange is they didn't ask," Howard answered and furrowed his brow while he thought about it. "He asked about you though."

"He did? Why? What did he say?"

"He wanted to know if I'd noticed you acting a bit off lately. Stuff like that."

"What did you tell him?"

"I told him no. Then he asked how it was that you found the burnt bush in the woods and the visiting room. I told him I didn't know."

"But you were with me when *we* found the bush."

"Yeah, but I didn't find the ribbon."

"Did you tell him about that?"

"No. I didn't think of it."

Just then the clap from the wooden block at the head table signaled it was time for them to serve. Charlie could not stop thinking about what Howard told him while he made his rounds. He was so distracted that he almost spilled the pitcher of milk, earning him a terse, "Watch it!" from Rick. When he finally sat down to eat, he was no longer hungry. His stomach felt like it was a knot.

"Do you think they'll want to talk to me?" he whispered to Howard.

"Probably," Howard answered.

"What are you two talking about?" Rick asked.

"Oh, those detective guys," Howard answered.

"Did you have your interview today?"

"It wasn't an interview," Howard corrected Rick. "It was an interrogation."

"Well, excuse me," Rick said a bit annoyed. "Seems like

they're talking to everyone."

"Not everyone," Howard corrected Rick again. "Just the boys who were here during the summer. Don't look so disappointed. If you want, I can tell them you did it. Then you can talk to them."

"Don't be funny."

"I'm not."

"So, they will be talking to me," Charlie said, sounding worried. "Why would they think I did it?"

"I don't think they do," Howard tried to sound positive. "They're just trying to find out who it is."

Charlie looked across the table at Gus. It was obvious he was listening to them, but was trying to act normal.

"So, have they talked to you yet?"

Gus looked at Charlie, his mouth open to take another bite of his meatloaf. Suddenly his hand trembled, and he put his fork down.

"No," he answered.

"It'll be okay," Charlie tried to reassure him. "No one has brought your name up."

Gus looked at him, then Howard with a confused expression. "Why would they?" he asked.

"No reason," Howard spoke up, giving Charlie a stern look. "Just forget about it and eat your dinner."

Gus stared at the two of them suspiciously, and slowly returned to eating his dinner. Charlie watched him for a while, noting that Gus's hand still shook.

After the dessert was finished and the tables were cleared, Howard and Charlie took their seats again. Father Mark stood behind his chair.

"I know that many of you have been asking when we will be moving into the new residence building. I have the answer for you," he said.

Howard glanced over his shoulder at Charlie and grinned.

"As you are all aware, due to the fire on the second floor and the smoke damage on the third, the seminarians have been occupying the building. It has been decided that we will not be moving."

Immediately the room filled with disappointed groans. Father Mark raised his hands and silenced everyone.

"Instead, the seminary will be permanently moving into the new building. After the dedication ceremony this Sunday, it will be known as Saint Francis Xavier Hall.

"Are there any questions?"

Immediately Rick's hand went up. Father Mark ignored it and turned toward Saint Peter table.

"Yes, Master DeVries."

Kenneth stood up beside his chair. "Have the police figured out who set the fire yet?"

"No, but they are still investigating it. Yes, Master Wilson."

Ted stood. "Is the curfew still in affect?"

"Yes, it is," Father Mark answered and turned toward the rest of the students. "And just to be clear, no one is permitted outside after the evening meal. And after lights out, you are all to remain in your beds. Your prefects will continue their nightly bed checks. This is an extremely serious matter, and it is for your protection."

With no other hands to call on, Father Mark relented. "Master Walters."

Rick stood beside his chair. "I understand the police won't be interrogating any of the students, just the resident boys who were here during the summer. Why is that?"

Father Mark glanced to his right at Brother Simon, then

back at Rick. "The detectives have their reasons. If you have any more questions, Master Walters, please see Brother Simon."

Rick sat back down.

After the prayer, the boys were dismissed, and quietly filed into the hall. As Charlie passed in front of the head table, Brother Simon stepped forward.

"Master MacCready, I'd like a word with you please."

"I'll catch up with you later," Charlie quickly told Howard.

"Okay," he answered.

Brother Simon led Charlie away from the other boys to a quiet corner of the refectory. He tucked his hands out of sight beneath his robes, and straightened his back. The look on his face was serious and stony.

"I've just been informed that the detectives would like a word with you tomorrow morning. Instead of your first period class, you will go to the visiting room next to Abbot Ambrose's office."

"Okay," Charlie answered with a nod. He could feel his stomach tighten again.

"Charlie, you have nothing to worry about," Brother Simon tried to reassure him. "I know you are not responsible for the fires. I'm sure they just want to see if you now who is."

Charlie thought for a moment. The knots in his stomach tightened some more. He looked away for a moment, debating whether or not to say anything. "Brother Simon, there's something I need to tell you."

Brother Simon looked past Charlie as the last of the prefects left the refectory. They were alone.

"What is it?"

"The day that Howard and I discovered the burned bush in the woods by the candle studio I found something."

Brother Simon cocked his head as he listened. "Go on," he

urged.

"In class we made beeswax candles and tied them together with a straw ribbon. We each had a different colored ribbon. Well, under a bush near the burnt one I found a ribbon. It was Gus's ribbon. I put it in my pocket because I didn't want Gus to get in trouble and sent away. I thought we could get through to him. Get him to stop before...."

"Anything serious happened?" Brother Simon continued Charlie's thought. "Master MacCready, I don't know what to say. Master Miller knows about this, I take it?"

"Yes, Brother."

"Well, this does not look good. In fact, this looks very bad for Master Kugele. I will need to talk with the Abbot. Is there anything else I should know?"

Charlie thought for a moment. "No."

"Then you may go."

~§~

That night, Charlie tossed and turned in his bed, unable to sleep. He could not stop thinking about his upcoming appointment with the detectives. At breakfast, he picked at his food, unable to eat. While he and Howard wheeled the dish cart into the kitchen, Charlie absentmindedly dropped a milk glass. It shattered on the floor.

"You have to calm down," Howard told him.

"I know. I'm just nervous."

"There's nothing to worry about. We don't know anything for sure."

"But what if they ask me about the fire in the woods? About the ribbon?"

"They don't know about that, so don't say anything."

"I guess you're right," Charlie nodded and swept the shards of glass into the dustpan.

While Howard and the other boys headed off to class, Charlie stood staring down the hall toward the visiting room. As he drew nearer, he could see the door was open, and heard the detective and Father Mark talking.

Father Mark looked up right as Charlie stepped into the doorway. He smiled and held out his hand.

"Come in, Master MacCready," he greeted. "This is Detective Johnstone."

"Hello, Charlie. Is it okay if I call you Charlie?"

"Yes sir."

"Please have a seat," Father Mark instructed. "I've just been telling Detective Johnstone that I will be staying with you this morning while he asks his questions."

Charlie smiled and let out a shaky sigh. He looked at the room. The coffee table and loveseat had been moved against the back wall. A folding table and two chairs were set in the center of the room. Charlie sat down with his back to the door. He felt a little less nervous knowing that Father Mark would be staying.

Charlie watched as the detective set a small tape recorder in the center of the table. He plugged a long cord into the back of the recorder and set the small microphone on the table in front of Charlie. He popped the recorder open and slipped a new cassette inside. He pressed a button and a small red light came on.

"Do you mind if I record our conversation?" he asked.

Charlie looked at Father Mark, who shrugged his shoulders and shook his head.

"No, I guess not," Charlie answered.

"Good," Detective Johnstone answered and sat down in the chair across from Charlie. "I understand that you and Howard

Miller were the two who discovered the fire in the woods last summer?"

Charlie nodded.

"Please, answer with your voice."

"Yes sir, we did."

"Very good. I understand that you waited by the site while Master Miller went to get help?"

"Yes sir."

"What did you do while he was gone?"

"Nothing."

"Did you look around?"

"Yes."

"Did you find anything out of the ordinary?"

Charlie thought for a moment. "No, nothing unusual."

"Now, what about the fire in the visiting room across the hall? When did you first notice it?"

"I didn't," Charlie answered. "I mean, at the time I didn't. I was on my way to dinner and I noticed the room was full of smoke. I thought it was just the wind blowing the smoke from the field burning inside. It wasn't until a few weeks later when I found out about the pig barn fire that I suspected there could have been an actual fire in that room."

"I see." Detective Johnstone bent down and picked something up off the floor. He set it on the table in front of Charlie. "Have you seen this before?"

Charlie looked at the box and read the name on the end. "Yes," he answered.

"This was the box you used to put your completed candles in last summer, isn't it?"

"Yes," Charlie answered, confused.

"When was the last time you saw it?"

"On the last day of candle making, I guess."

"That would be kind of hard since it has been in Abbot Ambrose's office since the fire in the visiting room."

"I—I don't understand," Charlie looked at Father Mark. From the look on the dean's face, Charlie knew he was as surprised as him.

"This box was left behind by the person who started the fire in the visiting room."

Charlie shook his head. "But I put my candles in my box on the last day of class."

"Perhaps the box was switched," Father Mark suggested.

"Father, please!" Detective Johnstone snapped angrily.

"I don't know how it got there. I never went into the room until the day I found out about the pig barn fire. Brother Owen caught me. I had to do work crew. You can ask him."

"We're not interested in that. What we want to know is how this got into the room."

"I told you I don't know," Charlie answered. He looked at Father Mark. "I don't want to answer any more questions."

Father Mark nodded. "I think we are finished here."

The detective switched off the tape recorder.

"Very well," he said coldly. "You may go."

Charlie started to stand up, but his knees were trembling and he fell back down in his chair. Father Mark grabbed his arm and pulled him gently to his feet.

"Are you okay?" he asked.

"Y-yes," Charlie answered feeling the strength return to his legs.

"Why don't you go back to your dorm and lie down. You may skip your classes this morning."

"Okay," Charlie answered, and slowly left the room. He paused for a moment and leaned against the wall outside the door.

"What was that all about?" Father Mark snapped at the detective.

"I was about to ask you the same thing."

"I don't know what you are trying to pull here, Detective Johnstone, but these theatrics are unwarranted. You are dealing with children here, not a bunch of criminals."

"Am I?"

Charlie pushed away from the wall and returned to his dorm.

HALLOWEEN

"Where've you been?" Howard asked when Charlie rushed into the dorm.

"After I finished reading to Father Cecil, I stopped in to see how Father Ignatius was coming with the museum. I guess I lost track of time."

"Well you better hurry and get into your costume."

For the first time Charlie noticed what Howard was wearing. He was dressed completely in black, black shoes, black slacks, black t-shirt.

"What are you supposed to be?"

"You'll see," Howard answered. "Here, help me with this." He pulled out a black turtleneck shirt that had two extra arms sewn onto each side. On its back was a red hourglass shape. Charlie held the shirt while Howard slipped it over his head.

"What are you supposed to be?" Charlie asked.

"A black widow spider," Howard answered and held up his arms. A piece of fishing line was attached to the arms so when Howard raised his hands, all the arms did the same. "You like it?"

Charlie stepped back and shivered. "Yeah, it's creepy enough. How'd you come up with that?"

"Brother Gregory helped me, but it was my idea. So, what are you going as?"

Charlie shrugged. "I wasn't going to dress up this year."

"Oh, you have to! I heard some of the guys talking and this year the dorm that has the most people in costume wins a special prize."

"But I can't think of anything."

"Rick!" Howard shouted.

"What?" came his distant response.

"Get over here, I need your help."

"Alright."

When Rick rounded the partition that separated the last cubicle from the lockers, Howard's and Charlie's mouths dropped open in shock.

"You can't go dressed like that!" Howard snapped.

"Why not?"

"Do you know what Dougary and his goons are going to do if you show up like that?"

"I don't care, it's a costume. What do you want?" Rick asked putting an end to Howard's protesting.

"You need to help Charlie with a costume."

"Me? Why me?"

"Because I still have to put on my make-up and you're," Howard frowned as he looked Rick over, "already dressed."

Rick looked at Charlie and folded his arms over his chest, flattening his padding. "Fine. Come on."

~§~

Eerie music with howling cats and cackling witches filled

the hallway outside the refectory. Howard smiled when he noticed Charlie had taken his place in line behind him.

"Much better," he said approvingly.

"It won't win any prizes for best costume, but it's okay," Charlie admitted. "It was either come as a hobo or—"

Just then the boys from Saint Peter started whistling and making a lot of noise. Charlie and Howard turned to see the reason.

Rick threw back his head and tossed the long blonde hair of his wig off his shoulders. He stuck out his chest, which was stuffed with two sponges, and strutted over to his place in line.

Howard shook his head.

"It's Halloween," Charlie said, in Rick's defense.

"Tell that to Dougary tomorrow."

"Where's Gus?" Charlie asked.

"Yeah, he has to wait tables tonight."

The refectory doors opened and fog bellowed into the hallway. Father Mark, dressed as Dracula, emerged.

"Velcome," he greeted, nearly spitting his fangs out. "Dinner is served."

The boys followed him into the darkened dining hall. Candles and jack-o-lanterns flickered down the center of each table. Red lights from the ceiling fixtures cast a dim glow across the disappearing fog on the floor. Behind the head table, the curtain was replaced with a wooden backdrop painted to look like a stone wall of a castle.

The prefects stood behind their chairs. Father Vicar was dressed in a black shirt, black slacks, and a black cape. His face looked paler than usual, which made his eyes appear more sunken. He threw back his head and opened his mouth slightly letting what appeared to be blood ooze out of the corners and down his face and neck. The sight caused Charlie to shudder, which appeared to please the monk.

Brother Owen was made up to like a zombie. If Charlie looked at him too much, he was sure he would not be able to eat his dinner, and he was looking forward to pizza tonight.

Brother Conrad was wrapped up in dirty white bandages, making him look even thinner than usual. He makes a good mummy, Charlie thought.

Brother Simon was dressed in a long black suit coat and top hat with a large black feather. It reminded Charlie of the pictures of undertakers in early 1900's New Orleans he saw in his World Cultures.

After the prayer, more haunting music played. Charlie watched as the waiters emerged from the kitchen carrying large pizza trays. The waiters were all dressed the same, in white shirts with long white aprons like deli workers wore. Their faces looked a little pale but not too unusual. It was not until Charlie saw the boy serve the head table that he cringed. A meat cleaver was embedded in the waiter's back. Bright red theatrical blood stained the white shirt. Charlie wondered how the boy made the cleaver stay in place. He watched Gus, eyeing his costume carefully to see if he could figure it out.

"Great costume, Gus," Howard said above the din.

"Thanks," Gus said, without a smile. "It can be a pain."

"I bet," Howard laughed.

After dinner, the members of the Halloween committee announced this year's festivities. Apples on strings hung from the ceiling, a twist to the bobbing for apples game. A jack-o-lantern piñata was brought out and readied in front of the head table. In the back of the refectory, along the wall, members of the committee revealed a long table filled with caramel apples, orange tinted popcorn balls, platters of cupcakes, pastries and a large punch bowl with witch's brew.

Charlie and Howard grabbed a cup of brew and headed to a quieter corner.

"This party is so lame," Howard groused. "All because of those stupid fires."

"Yeah," Charlie agreed.

"You hear any more from that detective guy?"

"No and I hope I never do again."

"Is Father Cecil still not talking to you?"

"Nah, he's over it. We talk a lot now."

"That's good," Howard said, sounding bored with the small talk. He watched Dougary and his thugs try to bite the apples hanging from the ceiling. No one was having any success. "You wanna give it a try?"

Charlie watched for a moment. "Sure, why not."

"Okay, here's the plan," Howard said. He whispered into Charlie's ear. "Got it?"

A smile spread across Charlie's lips. "Yeah."

They made their way over to the boy in charge of the game.

"So, what are the rules?" Howard asked.

"Just keep your hands clasped behind your back. That's all."

Howard nodded to Charlie. "Okay."

The two waited their turn before they walked into the ring of students. Howard scoped out an apple. "This one," he said to Charlie.

Charlie stood on one opposite side of the apple. At the same time, the boys leaned in and trapped the apple between them. Howard bit the apple, then grabbed it and pulled it free of the string.

"Cheaters!" Travis yelled and pointed at them. "That's not fair!"

"Hey, we followed the rule, no hands." He looked at the

boy in charge.

"That's right," he agreed. "Congratulations!" He handed Howard a brown paper sack.

Howard took it and headed back to his quiet corner. Charlie followed. Together they watched Travis and Austin Fulton gang up on an apple. The apple slipped and the boys' faces crashed into each other in a strange, open-mouthed kiss. Immediately, they jumped back and their hands wiped their faces. Howard and Charlie roared with laughter.

"Say, have you seen Gus?" Charlie asked when he regained his composure.

Howard looked around. "No, I haven't. Maybe he's in the kitchen. Come on."

Just as the two entered the kitchen, the back door opened and Gus walked inside.

"Where've you been?" Howard asked.

"I went outside to throw some garbage out," Gus answered in an annoyed tone.

"How'd you get so dirty?" Charlie asked looking at Gus's soiled white shirt and apron.

Gus looked at his clothes and opened his mouth to speak just as the fire siren began to blare.

The three boys quickly returned to the refectory where the music had stopped. The boys, some covering their ears due to the loud high-pitched siren, formed a line.

"You will follow Brother Conrad and exit the building. Gather on the Great Lawn by your dorm groups," Father Mark instructed.

Howard, Charlie, and Gus quickly joined the line. Silently they followed the others down the hall toward the foyer.

The air was thick with the smell of burning rubber. Charlie covered his nose and mouth with his sleeve as he stepped through the main doors of the Abbey. He looked across the Great Lawn and saw a flickering glow in the distance. Suddenly, he realized the garage was on fire.

The sound of sirens filled the night and grew louder as the fire engines roared up the hill. Charlie huddled with the members of Saint Nicholas dorm. From their post, they had a clear view of the blaze.

A group of monks hurried across the lawn toward the garage completely engulfed in flames. Charlie recognized Abbot Ambrose immediately. He silently said a prayer that his great-uncle would be safe.

"What do you suppose started it?"

Charlie looked beside him. "How should I know?" he said, giving Kenneth a disgusted look. "Shouldn't you be with your dorm?"

"Can't see the fire from over there," he answered, his eyes fixed on the glow in the distance. "Say, I hear you have a Saint Christopher medal."

Charlie's head instantly turned to look at Kenneth and his hand went over his chest, feeling the key, locket and medal beneath his shirt. "Who says?"

"How much do you want for it? Name your price. I'll give you anything."

"It's not for sale," Charlie answered coldly, but inside he was shaking.

"Suit yourself, but I always get what I want."

"Not this time," Charlie said, and walked away. He spotted Howard standing alone, away from the others.

"What a freak!" he said when he walked up to Howard.

"Who?"

"DeVries. He just asked me to sell him my Saint Christopher medal."

Howard looked at Charlie. "How did he find out about that?"

"Three guesses and the first two don't count," Charlie answered and looked around for Gus.

"Don't worry about it." Howard shook his head and returned to staring at the fire.

"You know, he also asked me what I thought started the fire. He seems a little obsessed, don't you think?" Charlie shook his head, still disgusted.

"I think you mean, possessed," Howard added with a self-satisfied laugh. "Forget about him," he said dismissively, continuing to stare at something in the distance.

Charlie looked around to see what Howard was watching and realized he was not staring at the fire. The boys from their dorm were huddled in small clusters behind them, toward the Abbey, except for Gus. Charlie spotted him a few yards in front of them. He was knelt down, sitting on his feet by a tree. His arms were wrapped around himself in a self-hug. The meat cleaver still stuck in his back shook while he cried.

"What's wrong with Gus?"

"I don't know," Howard answered. "When we came outside, he kept saying, 'No, no, no.' He walked over there and…."

"Should we go to him?"

"No," Howard answered. He turned and looked at Charlie. "Taking the garbage out? I know Gus is a klutz but even he couldn't get that dirty doing that. Besides, his shirt had dirt on it. Dirt like you get going through the tunnel."

Charlie's eyes widened. "You don't think…."

"I wish I didn't," Howard answered.

"We need to tell Brother Simon or Father Mark."

"Not just yet. They have their hands full already. Let me

talk to Gus first."

"Howard, we can't keep this quiet. We will be in so much trouble."

"I know. I'll talk to him tonight, just not now."

"May I have your attention?" Father Mark shouted from the front steps of the Abbey. "The fire department has everything under control. You should all return to your dorms and get ready for lights out."

A groan rose from the boys of Saint Peter. Their protests were met with a stern look from Father Vicar.

Charlie sat on his bed staring out at the flashing lights across the Great Lawn. The glow of the fire had died down. Thoughts of Kenneth flashed in his mind. Never before had he felt so uneasy around another schoolmate.

"Well, that got nowhere."

Charlie looked at Howard. His face was clean again. No more black makeup. "So, he's not talking?"

"Actually, he did. He claims he went out to throw away the garbage and saw someone sneaking off to the tunnel. He said he followed but without a light, lost him. So he came back."

"They still out there?" Howard asked. He craned his neck to see out the window while he sat on his bed.

Charlie glanced out the window. The lights were still flashing. "Yeah," he answered. "But I think the fire is out. So are we going to tell Father Mark?"

"It can wait 'til morning."

Sleep was nearly impossible for Charlie. He stared at the ceiling and listened to the creaking springs of the beds around him. It was plain the other boys were having just as much trouble.

Suddenly the siren blared and the lights came on. Charlie leapt from his bed and was in the center of the dorm with the other boys when the doors opened. Brother Simon entered with his hands raised in the air. Then the siren stopped.

"It's okay," he assured the boys. "It was a false alarm."

"What happened," one of the older boys asked.

"One of the brothers accidently tripped the circuit when he was resetting the alarm system. Go back to bed. Everything is okay."

Charlie followed Howard back to their cubicle. He was not as sure everything was okay as Brother Simon but he climbed back into his bed anyway.

Charlie woke up the next morning to the sun shining in his window. He sat up and looked around the dorm. Rick was still fast asleep with his covers pulled over his head. Howard lay facing the partition, his back to Charlie. He glanced at the clock on Howard's nightstand. It was eight o'clock.

The doors opened. Brother Simon entered and walked around the dorm, waking the boys up gently.

"Good morning, Master MacCready," he greeted Charlie. "We're going to have a late breakfast in a half an hour. So, get showered and dressed."

The refectory was filled with the usual chatter as the boys ate their breakfast. Charlie eyed Gus across the table. Gus appeared unaffected by the previous night's fire and false alarm. He sat eating his breakfast as usual, syrup dripping from his chin.

After the tables were cleared, Father Mark walked around to the front of the head table. His face belied how tired he felt. Charlie figured the sleep-in was as much for the prefects and dean as it was for them.

"Normally Abbot Ambrose would be here to announce the new members of the Altar Boys Club. Unfortunately, he is tied up with the business of the fire last night, so there will be no announcement at present.

"Last night's fire destroyed the garage as well as three of the Abbey's vehicles. We are lucky their gas tanks did not explode or it would have been much worse.

"I can't stress this enough, whoever is doing this needs to step forward now and put a stop to this before someone gets hurt."

Charlie detected a note of anger in Father Mark's tone. He looked across the table at Gus. Gus sat staring at the Saint Peter table.

"I assure you, if you do not and these fires continue you will be prosecuted. I will be in my office all day.

"Classes will begin two hours late today. Immediately following the announcements, we will have Mass in the lounge area on the fourth floor. Do not be late. We will be taking roll."

THE POLYGRAPH TEST

"I can't believe Father Mark didn't talk to Gus right away," Charlie lamented while he stood looking out the north window of the bell tower. The autumn breeze felt cold against his cheeks. He wrapped his coat tighter around him and tucked his hands into his sleeves.

"He said he already knew about it," Howard explained.

"How?"

"How should I know? Maybe Gus talked to him on his own." Howard shrugged while he stared at the charred remains of the garage in the distance.

"So now what?"

"Rumor has it the police are going to start doing polygraph tests on some of the resident boys."

"What's that?" Charlie asked.

"It's a lie detector. They have a machine that supposedly can tell when a person is lying."

"Wow," Charlie breathed. "So why us? Why not the students and the seminarians?"

"Because they weren't here when the first fires happened.

They feel positive it was one of the resident boys."

Charlie turned away from the view. "Do you think we could be wrong about Gus? I mean, maybe he's telling the truth and really did see someone."

Just then Gus poked his head up through the trap door opening.

"Howard, Father Mark wants you right away. He's in the visiting room next to his office."

Charlie looked at Howard and felt a sinking in his stomach.

"Guess I better go," he said. "See you later."

Gus stepped into the belfry and let Howard pass. He stood looking down through the opening. "I heard what you said."

Charlie felt his face turning red from embarrassment at being caught. "Gus, I—"

"I can't believe you actually think I'm the one behind the fires." He turned and looked at Charlie.

"Howard and I know about the cigarettes."

"Know what?"

"That you're smoking," Charlie whispered.

"Smoking!" Gus shouted. "I am not!"

"But I saw Kenneth give them to you down there by the grotto; and, and, I saw them drop out of your pocket in class, remember?"

Gus shook his head. "I was taking them away from him. I told Kenneth if he got caught with them or worse, smoking, he would be in so much trouble. I wasn't smoking."

"But Father Cecil and I smelled it on your clothes."

"Because I was around Kenneth when *he* was smoking. I was not smoking; and I am not the one setting the fires either," Gus said emphatically. "I know I haven't been the most fun to be around lately but I would never do such a thing. As much as I hate it here, this is the only home I've got."

"I'm sorry, Gus."

"Forget about it," Gus said and walked over to the north window. "I really did try to stop him."

"Him? So you know who's setting the fires?" Charlie asked.

"No. I never saw his face."

"But you have an idea?"

"I wish I did," Gus answered.

"So, what does Father Mark want with Howard?"

"I don't know."

Charlie turned and looked out the window again.

"I can't believe the police are still digging through the ashes over there. They've been at it for two weeks. What do they think they'll find?"

Gus shrugged.

Charlie looked at Gus. "So, does this mean we're back to being friends?"

Gus nodded. Charlie smiled. They stood watching the scene in the distance until it was almost time for lunch. They left the bell tower before the Angelus rang.

The hallway outside the refectory was quiet when they took their places in line. Howard was already standing in his spot, staring at the back of the boy's head in front of him.

"What happened?" Charlie whispered over Howard's shoulder.

Howard shook his head.

The doors opened and the boys filed inside. After the prayer the boys sat down. Charlie looked at the head table. Brother Simon was seated next to Father Mark and the two had their heads together, talking about something. Occasionally they glanced in the boys' direction.

"So, what did Father Mark want?" Charlie asked again.

"I had to take a polygraph test," Howard admitted quietly.

"You did?"

"Sh-h-h!" Howard hissed nervously, looking at the head table, then turning toward Charlie.

"What? Sorry," Charlie whispered.

"I'm not supposed to talk about it."

"Why not?"

"Because they're still testing other guys."

"Do you know who else?"

"No, but when I left, DeVries was going in."

Gus looked up. "Kenneth?"

Howard looked across the table at Gus. "Yeah," he answered eyeing Gus curiously. "Does that matter?"

"No," Gus shrugged. "Just surprised is all."

"So, what was it like?" Charlie asked.

"There were two detectives in the room with Father Mark. The one guy who seemed to be in charge had me sit in a chair in front of a table in the center of the room. The other guy was sitting behind the table turning some knobs on a metal thing about the size of a suitcase.

"The guy in charge explained what they were going to do and that it wouldn't hurt. He strapped a belt around my chest. Then the guy sitting over the contraption told me to sit still, look straight ahead and not move. Then they asked me a bunch of yes-or-no questions. I was so nervous."

"What did they ask you?"

"At first, they verified my name and how old I am, stuff like that. Then they started asking me questions about the fires. If I knew who was setting them. They even asked me if I was setting them. Can you believe that?"

"How do you think you did?" Charlie asked.

"I don't know. They wouldn't tell me. The guy asking the

questions kept looking at Father Mark whenever I answered."

"Well, I'm sure you did fine," Charlie tried to sound positive.

When lunch concluded, Father Mark stood. He gripped the back of his chair while looked around the room and took a deep breath. "I would like to see the following boys before you leave, Master Miller, Master Kuegle, and Master Wilson."

Howard turned and looked at Charlie.

Charlie could see the fear in his friend's eyes. "Don't worry. It's going to be okay," he whispered.

"But what—"

"Please join me in prayer," Father Mark said, silencing Howard.

After the prayer, Charlie told Howard, "I'll wait for you in the hall." He followed the other boys out of the refectory and watched Father Mark close the doors.

Charlie looked at the clock on the wall and began to pace. He was sure it was nothing. The refectory door opened and Ted Wilson came out.

"Was that about the results of your polygraph?" Charlie asked.

"Yes," Ted answered. "I passed, thank God."

That's great," Charlie exclaimed. "What about Howard and Gus?"

"Don't know. Father Mark is telling us individually."

"Oh," Charlie said, feeling the butterflies in his stomach spring to life. "Ted, can I ask you a question?"

"Sure, but make it fast. I have to be somewhere."

"Why did you ask to be moved out of Saint Nicholas?"

Ted looked bewildered. "I didn't ask to move. Father Abbot asked me to. He wants me to keep an eye on the younger members of Saint Peter."

"So, it wasn't your idea?"

"Hell, no. I've gotta go."

Charlie watched Ted head up the stairs and then he resumed his pacing.

After another five minutes, the door opened again and Gus came out. Charlie stopped. "And?" he said, eagerly.

"I told you I wasn't the one lighting the fires," he said.

"I believe you," Charlie said.

"But you had your doubts."

"At first and I'm sorry."

"Forget it," Gus said.

"How do you think Howard did?"

"I don't know, but he's a nervous wreck," Gus answered, looking over his shoulder at the refectory doors. "I'll have to find out later. I have to go."

Alone once again, Charlie looked at the clock. He had ten minutes before Father Cecil expected him. With his anxiety growing with each tick on the clock, Charlie began pacing again.

The doors opened. Charlie stopped. Father Mark walked into the hallway with his arm around Howard's shoulders. He stopped and looked at Charlie.

"Shouldn't you be with Father Cecil?" he said.

"Yes, Father," Charlie stammered. "I just wanted to make sure Howard was okay."

"I'm fine, Charlie," Howard said, though his tone belied his words.

"Well, remember what I said," Father Mark said to Howard.

"I will."

"Good. Now, Brother Gregory will be wondering where you are. You best run along."

Charlie waited until Father Mark was on his way to his office, before he looked at Howard. "So?"

A worried expression came over Howard. "I failed the polygraph test."

"You did? How is that possible?"

"Father Mark said being nervous could cause a false reading. So he said the police want to retest me."

"When?"

"I'm supposed to meet with them again this afternoon, after my visit with Brother Gregory."

~§~

The afternoon sun was bright and its warmth felt good against Charlie's face as he helped Father Cecil down the front steps of the Abbey's main entrance. They turned east, heading toward their usual walking route past the swimming pool and pig barns.

"So, what's troubling you?" Father Cecil asked.

Charlie looked at him curiously. "What makes you think something's bothering me?"

"Because every time you are troubled by something, you sigh a lot."

"Oh," Charlie answered and looked back at the path, suddenly self-conscious and aware of his breathing. "After lunch I found out Howard failed his lie detector test. The police are testing him again and questioning him about the fires."

"I see."

"But he isn't doing it," Charlie insisted.

"You're positive about that?"

"Yes, Father. I am."

"Then do you know who is?"

"No, but I have my suspicions."

"Your friend Gus?"

"No, not any longer. He passed his lie detector test."

"I see," Father Cecil nodded. "What's that sound?" he asked and stopped.

Charlie looked at the men working in the grotto of Our Lady of the Subway. They had moved the life-size statue out of her nook and were sealing the entrance to the tunnel. He relayed what was happening to Father Cecil.

"Well, it was bound to happen sooner or later," he nodded. "It should have been done a long time ago."

"I sort of liked the tunnel," Charlie admitted.

"I'm sure you did." Father Cecil smiled.

As the two rounded the path near the swimming pool Charlie jumped.

"What is it?" Father Cecil asked.

"Oh, nothing," Charlie answered. "I was just startled."

"Hey, MacCready," Kenneth greeted, seemingly surprised himself, and acting a bit nervous. He stepped away from a large tree and onto the path. "Hi, Father."

"So, what were you doing?" Charlie asked looking at the tree, then back at Kenneth.

"Nothing. Hey, have you thought about my offer?"

"No. I already told you, it's not for sale."

"We'll see. See you later."

Charlie clenched his teeth and scowled at the back of Kenneth's head.

"Who was that and what was that all about?" Father Cecil asked.

"That was Kenneth DeVries," Charlie answered. "The night of the fire, he said he wanted to buy my Saint Christopher medal."

Charlie felt Father Cecil's hand tighten its grip on his arm.

"Charlie, how did he find out about the medal?"

"I don't know for sure, but I suspect Gus told him. Gus was there when I opened the present from my grandma."

"Does Gus know about the etching on the back?"

"No, I don't think so. Only Howard has seen it."

"Charlie you mustn't show it to anyone or tell anyone about it."

"But why?"

"I can't say," Father Cecil answered.

"That's what everyone keeps saying. Why won't anyone tell me what is going on?"

"In time, Charlie. In time," Father Cecil said, nodding to himself. "Shall we continue our walk?"

"Okay," Charlie answered, less than enthused.

CHRISTMAS

The Great Lawn was blanketed in white. The snow that started falling the night before continued to fall all morning. The view out the north arch of the bell tower reminded Charlie of one of his grandmother's snow globes. He turned away from the winter scene and sat on the floor. He pulled a letter from the pocket of his coat and began reading quietly.

"I can't wait until Christmas," Gus said excitedly, leaning out of the window opening and trying to catch a falling snowflake.

"Be careful!" Howard snapped. He grabbed Gus's belt and tugged him back. "You fall and you'll miss Christmas all together."

"I won't fall," Gus said. He walked across the belfry to the south archway.

Howard looked at Charlie and lowered his voice to a whisper. "So, did your grandma say anything about the writing on the back of your medal?"

"No." Charlie shook his head. "I didn't think she would. I sure would like to know why DeVries wants it so bad. I'm still afraid he might try to steal it."

"Are we even sure he knows about the stuff on the back?"

"No. I wish there were a way to find out though."

Howard leaned against the wall between the south and east window. He pursed his lips and squinted while he thought. Suddenly, he grinned.

"I've got it!" he nearly shouted. He cringed and looked at Gus. Gus was too busy scraping the snow from the west window sill to notice. "Has DeVries ever seen your medal?" he whispered.

Charlie thought for a moment. "I don't think so."

"Perfect! What we need is another Saint Christopher medal. I saw one in a gift shop in town when Father Mark took me to get my new glasses last summer. Maybe it's still there or they have more? We can buy it and sell that one to DeVries. If he takes it then we will know he doesn't know anything."

"That's great, Howard. Only one problem, how are we going to get to town? We're not allowed off the hill, remember?"

"All right, so it's not perfect. I'll figure something out," Howard assured him. "Until then, if he asks about it again, tell him you're thinking about it."

"Okay."

"When we do get the new medal, we'll tell him we want three times what we paid for it." Howard grinned fiendishly.

Charlie thought about it and hesitantly shook his head. "I don't know, wouldn't that be stealing?"

"No. He told you to name your price, didn't he?"

"Yeah," Charlie nodded.

"Then you can ask anything you want. He doesn't have to buy it."

Again, Charlie thought for a moment. "Okay, we've got a

plan." He stuffed his letter into his pocket and stood up.

He looked out across the Great Lawn to where the garage stood.

"It's funny. With it covered in snow no one would ever know there was ever a fire."

"Don't remind me," Howard said.

Charlie looked at him. "So you failed the lie detector test twice. I know you aren't lying and so does Father Mark."

Howard shrugged. "I know but that detective guy bugs me. What if they pin it on me just to get it solved? I could end up in juvie."

"That's not going to happen," Charlie said confidently. "Look, there hasn't been a fire in two months. Maybe whoever was doing it got the message and stopped."

"Or maybe he's just waiting for another big moment. Come on, we better get out of here. Gus, leave the snow. It's almost time for the bells to ring."

The boys quickly left the belfry and closed the trap door behind them. When they reached the stairwell on the fourth floor, the bells began to chime.

"That was close," Gus said, his eyes wide and unblinking.

"We better get downstairs to lunch. Today we're having roast beef and I don't want to miss it," Howard said, and headed down the stairs. Charlie and Gus followed close behind.

After the lunch plates were cleared, Father Mark stood by his chair to make the announcements.

"Tomorrow is Christmas—" Applause immediately erupted. He smiled and let the boys have their moment, then raised his hands and silenced them again. "The Altar Boys need to spend a little extra time this afternoon with their brothers. Father Vicar has asked for volunteers to assist him with decorating the Abbey Church for midnight Mass. Those who wish to help, please see him in the hallway after dismissal. Our last announcement, any boys wishing to go to town this afternoon for some last-minute shopping, I will be taking the van and have room for about ten boys. Meet me out back at one."

Howard turned and looked at Charlie with an open-mouth smile. Charlie nodded his understanding and could not help but smile back.

"That concludes our announcements."

After the prayer the two met in the hall. Since Howard knew where the shop was, it was decided that he would go to town. Charlie gave him all the money his grandmother had given him and watched to be sure Howard got a seat in the van. He waved to Howard as the van pulled away.

The afternoon with Father Cecil seemed to drag on. Charlie did his usual chores of dusting and sweeping, being sure to put everything back in its proper place so Father Cecil would not trip or bump into it. He read out of Dickens for a while but his heart was not in it.

"What's wrong?" Father Cecil asked at one point.

Charlie took a deep breath. He remembered that Father Cecil could hear him sigh. He let it out slowly and as quietly as he could. "Just excited about tomorrow, I guess."

"I see." The priest smiled. "Is it still snowing outside?"

Charlie stretched his neck to see out the window beside Father Cecil's chair. The small panes of glass were fogged around the edges. Still Charlie could make out the tiny flakes still falling.

"Yes," he answered.

Father Cecil smiled. "I have always wanted a white Christmas. Ever since I was a child, I dreamed of it. Wouldn't you know it, I finally get one and I can't see it."

Charlie suddenly felt bad inside. He did not know what to say and the room fell silent.

"Hey, would you like to take a walk outside?" he finally offered. "I'll make sure you won't fall."

Father Cecil cocked his head and smiled. "That sounds wonderful. I haven't gone outside in the snow for a long time."

Moments later the two emerged from the front entrance and carefully walked down the steps. Charlie started to turn east, to take their usual route but Father Cecil stopped him.

"Let's go the other way."

"Okay," Charlie nodded.

"Tell me what you see."

As the two slowly walked along the freshly shoveled sidewalk, Charlie described the scene on the Great Lawn. Boys were laughing and throwing balls of snow at each other. Some were busy building a giant snowman. The boughs on the trees bent downward under the weight of the snow. Everything was white and looked so pretty.

"What's that?" Father Cecil suddenly stopped and turned his ear to listen.

Charlie looked around. He spotted Kenneth and a man standing in the distance standing beside a black car near the burned down garage. "It's just that guy Kenneth talking with someone."

"You mean, arguing."

Charlie listened. Father Cecil was right, they were arguing though Charlie could not make out about what.

"Isn't he the boy who is after your medal?"

"Yes," Charlie answered. "But he's not going to get it."

"That's good," Father Cecil said, nodding his approval. "Let's head back inside. Maybe we can get some hot cocoa in the refectory?"

"Sounds great!"

Charlie carefully helped Father Cecil back up the front steps and into the foyer. He took the priest's heavy wool cape and brushed off the melting snowflakes. Father Cecil led the way to the monastery's refectory. Charlie was surprised to see it was very much like the students' refectory. Long tables stretched out in front of the head table. To the right of the head table was a podium with a microphone attached. A large book, Charlie assumed was a Bible, lay open on the top. In the back of the refectory was a table. Three polished silver urns sat flanked by carefully stacked coffee mugs.

"I believe you will find the urn on the right has the hot cocoa," Father Cecil instructed. He pulled out a chair and sat down at the nearest table.

Sure enough, Charlie found the cocoa where Father Cecil said it would be. He poured a cup for the priest and carefully brought it to him.

"Don't be shy. Be sure to get yourself a cup. It's okay," Father Cecil assured him.

Charlie returned with his cup, and sat down beside his priest. He sipped his cocoa and looked around at the refectory some more. The walls were void of any décor. On the west wall was a row of stained-glass windows depicting various Bible scenes beginning with Adam and Eve in the Garden of Eden and ending with one that gave him the creeps: four riders on four horses. The first rider was a soldier on a red horse wielding a long sword. The second was sickly looking man on a dark horse and carrying a scale. The third was a skeleton on a pale horse with a black figure following it. The last rider was not so scary. It was a king on a white horse carrying a bow and arrow. Charlie stared at that window the longest wondering what it was about.

"How's your cocoa?" Father Cecil asked.

"It's good," Charlie answered, looking away from the window. "Where's your Christmas tree?"

Father Cecil smiled. "It's in our lounge."

"Don't you decorate in here too, like we do?"

"No. We keep it like it is. Simple and clean."

"Oh," Charlie nodded.

"Well, good to see you are out and about, Cecil," a monk greeted, walking up behind them. Charlie jumped and turned around.

The monk was one Charlie had not seen before. He was average height and build. His face was kind and he smiled. Charlie nodded to him.

"Who's your young friend?"

"This is Master MacCready," Father Cecil introduced. "Master MacCready, this is Brother Brian. He's in charge of our vineyards."

Charlie started to stand up but Brother Brian held up his hand, halting him.

"Pleased to meet you, Master MacCready."

Just then the bells in the tower chimed.

"Oh, looks like it's time for Vespers."

Father Cecil quickly drank the last of his cocoa.

"I'll take your cups," Brother Brian offered.

"Thank you," Charlie said. "Do you want me to help you to the Abbey Church?"

"No, Charlie, I can manage. Would you be so kind as to put my cape away for me, though?"

"Sure. It was nice meeting you, Brother Brian. Thank you for taking care of the cups."

"You too, Master MacCready."

Charlie quickly hung Father Cecil's cape in the closet of his cell, then returned to Saint Nicholas dorm. The closer he got to his dorm, the more excited he became. He hoped Howard was back and had the medal. They could then put their plan into action that night.

When he reached his cubicle, Howard was waiting. He jumped off his bed.

"It's about time!" he greeted Charlie.

"Did you get it?"

"Of course, but it took everything you gave me."

"That's okay," Charlie shrugged. "Let me see it."

Howard handed him a small white box. Charlie clumsily opened it, nearly dropping the medal.

"Wow! It's perfect. It looks just like mine, only newer."

"That's the idea," Howard reminded him. "Now, let's find Kenneth and give him the good news. He was in the lounge a few minutes ago. Maybe he's still there."

Charlie put the medal back in the box.

"You should probably leave the box behind. Just put the medal in your pocket."

"Right!" Charlie agreed.

The two walked into the student lounge across from the sinks and restrooms in the center of the student wing on the fourth floor. Sure enough, Kenneth was sitting on the window sill in the corner, staring out at something below.

Howard sat down in an empty chair and grabbed a magazine, pretending to read while he kept an eye on Charlie.

"Hey Kenneth," Charlie said quietly, looking over his shoulder.

Kenneth looked at him expressionless.

"Are you still interested in buying my Saint Christopher medal?"

Kenneth's eyes lit up and he jumped to his feet. "Yeah," he said excited.

"Well, it's gonna cost you."

"Name it."

"Twenty bucks," Charlie said nervously. He glanced over his shoulder, then back at Kenneth.

"Let's see it first."

"Okay, you can look but not touch." Charlie carefully pulled the medal from his pocket and opened his fist. To his relief the medal was face up.

Kenneth smiled and pulled out his wallet. When he opened it, Charlie noticed the thick stack of bills. Gus was right, he thought. Kenneth was rich!

"Here," Kenneth said, handing him a twenty. He grabbed the medal without looking at the back and rushed off.

As Charlie walked back to Howard, he could not help but grin. He held up the twenty-dollar bill, excited that their plan worked.

"Way to go!" Howard said, jumping to his feet.

"Half of this is yours since you did most of the work."

"Thanks. Now we need to watch him to see what he does," Howard said.

Kenneth rushed down the stairs to the first floor unaware that he was being followed. He slipped into an empty visiting room. Charlie and Howard stealthily crept to the edge of the doorway and listened. Kenneth dialed the telephone.

"I've got it!" he announced.

"Tomorrow? After lunch? Okay," he said and hung up the phone.

Charlie and Howard quickly ducked into the next visiting room, and waited until the coast was clear.

"What do you make of that?" Howard asked.

"I don't know," Charlie answered. "We'll have to watch."

The artificial pine tree in the center of the dorm looked less festive without the colorful twinkling lights. Still, Charlie thought it was pretty, and none of them seemed to mind when they woke to find the floor around it piled with brightly wrapped packages. The fires from the past months might have put out the lights, but they did not extinguish the boys' Christmas spirit.

Charlie sat on the sofa eating a gingerbread cookie and sipping his eggnog while he read a card from his grandmother. He smiled when he read how pleased she was with the candle he sent her. He made a mental note to thank Abbot Ambrose for helping him pack it.

"So, what did your grandma give you this year?" Howard asked, looking at the pile of unwrapped gifts in front of Charlie.

Charlie pulled on a gold chain until a watch popped out of his pocket. "A watch," he said proudly.

Howard grabbed the pocket watch and examined it closely.

"I don't think it works," Charlie said. "I wound it but nothing happened."

"Oh no, not another mystery!" Howard groaned. He handed the watch back to Charlie.

"No, it's not," Charlie shook his head. He popped the cover over the face open and held it out for Howard to see. "It was my grandfather's."

Howard leaned forward and looked at the watch.

"Good," he smiled, nodding his approval and relief. "No new mysteries to solve."

"Not that I can see."

"Don't forget, we need to tail 'you-know-who' after lunch," Howard lowered his voice and looked around.

Before lunch, Charlie gathered up his gifts and put them in a pile on the foot of his locker. He snapped his lock shut before heading downstairs with Howard.

Lunch was more like Christmas dinner. The smell of roast

turkey, baked ham, candied yams and freshly baked rolls filled the refectory. Charlie sat back in his chair and took a deep breath.

"I'm stuffed," Howard said. He pushed his empty plate toward the center of the table and took the last gulp of his milk.

"I can't eat another bite," Charlie agreed. He looked across the table at Gus. "Where do you put it all?" he asked.

"Wha—?" Gus said his mouth full of dressing and cranberry sauce.

"Oh, Gus! Close your mouth when you eat," Howard grimaced.

After the plates were cleared, the dessert was served. Charlie sat for a moment and looked at his slice of pumpkin pie topped with a mountain of whipped cream. He looked at Howard.

"I guess I can manage one little bite," he said before finishing off his dessert.

After the meal there were just a few announcements before the boys were dismissed.

While Kenneth retrieved his coat from Saint Peter dorm, Charlie kept a lookout from a safe distance.

"Here," Howard said, handing Charlie his coat. He slipped his own on while they waited for Kenneth to emerge from his dorm.

"Looks like we're going outside," Charlie said.

"Well, just in case, I brought these." Howard flashed his binoculars at Charlie.

"Good thinking."

Just then the dormitory doors opened and Kenneth entered the hallway.

"And we're off," Howard said.

The pair followed Kenneth down the stairs to the first floor and then out the front of the building.

"Wait!" Charlie said when they were about to start across the Great Lawn. "With all of this snow, he'll see us."

Howard thought for a moment. "You're right. To the bell tower!"

They rushed back into the Abbey and in minutes were standing in the belfry. Charlie squinted to see in the distance but the white snow-covered lawn was blinding. Howard had his binoculars pressed against his glasses while he looked out the north arch.

"There he is!" he announced. "He's pacing in the parking lot. The person he called must be late. Oh-oh, here comes a car. It's stopping. Someone's getting out. I think it must be his uncle. He's walking over to DeVries. DeVries is saying something to him. Boy, I wish we could hear. Now DeVries is handing him something, the medal, I think. Yeah, it's the medal. The man is looking it over. What? He just threw it on the ground. He's yelling at DeVries. Oh! He just slapped him really hard. Now he's getting back into his car. He's gone."

"Wow!" Charlie breathed. "What is Kenneth doing now?"

"He's picking up the medal and now he's heading back." Howard lowered his binoculars. "That was strange."

"I'll say." Charlie looked at his watch. "I've got to go see Father Cecil. I'll catch up with you later."

Charlie stopped by his dorm and grabbed the small, brightly wrapped gift from under the tree. He checked the tag, then rushed off to Father Cecil's room.

"Merry Christmas!" he greeted when the priest opened his door.

"Merry Christmas to you too, Charlie. Come on in."

When Charlie entered, he noticed there were tins of cookies, plates of fancy breads, boxes of chocolates and a pitcher of milk sitting on the table. Father Cecil ignored them and walked back to his chair in the corner.

"So, did you have a wonderful morning?"

"Yes," Charlie nodded. "I got a pocket watch from my grandmother. It doesn't work but it was my grandfather's. So, it's okay. Oh, here," he gasped and held out the gift. "I have something for you."

"You do?" Father Cecil questioned. A slight smile came to his lips.

Charlie gave the gift to him and sat down in the chair by the table to watch. Father Cecil felt the edges of the gift, feeling the neatly folded edges. He felt the ribbon and bow.

"Go ahead and open it," Charlie urged.

Father Cecil nodded. He tore the paper away and felt the gift. "A book?" he said with a smile.

"Not just any book," Charlie informed him. "Open it up."

Father Cecil carefully opened the book's cover. He ran his hand over the page and stopped. His mouth gaped.

"The Adventures of Oliver Twist," he said out loud. "How did you—where did you—"

"My grandma found it for me. I told her all about you and that I wanted to get you something for Christmas. I told her about your Bible. She found the book."

"It's perfect, Charlie. Thank you."

Suddenly a siren blasted. Charlie jumped to his feet, knocking the chair over. He picked it up and put it back in its place.

"Charlie, grab my cape."

Charlie retrieved the heavy wool cape from the closet and put it over Father Cecil's shoulders. The priest fastened the large button securely at his neck and held out his hand. Charlie quickly took Father Cecil's hand and put it on his shoulder. The two entered the hallway.

"Go to the left," Father Cecil instructed. "The fire escape is at the end of the hall."

"Are you okay, Father?" a monk asked as he passed them.

"Yes," he answered over the noise.

"This can't be happening," Charlie said. "Not today. Not on Christmas."

"Keep moving, Charlie. We'll be okay."

When Charlie opened the outside door a blast of cold air hit him. He wished he had his coat. Carefully, he guided Father Cecil down the steps and over to the Great Lawn.

"I'll take it from here," another monk said. "You should join your dorm mates."

"Yes, Brother," Charlie said. "I'll see you later, Father."

"Be safe," Father Cecil called after him.

Charlie immediately spotted Gus standing with a group of boys trying to keep warm. He hurried over to them.

"What's going on?" he asked, joining the huddle.

"I don't know," Gus answered.

"Where's Howard?"

"I haven't seen him since lunch."

Charlie looked at the other boys. Kenneth was missing too. He looked at the main entrance just as Abbot Ambrose stepped out.

"It's all right," he announced. "You may all return to your dorms."

The boys did not hesitate. They rushed the front entrance in the hopes of getting warm. Charlie and Gus hurried up the stairs back to their dorm.

"I can't believe it," Charlie said and opened the door. "You'd think since it's Christmas that whoever is doing this would give it a rest."

Charlie stopped and looked at his bed. The blankets were pulled back and thrown on the floor. His pillow was torn, white feathers were everywhere. The drawer of his nightstand was pulled out and emptied on the floor. He turned to Gus.

"Get Brother Simon."

While Gus rushed off to find their prefect, Charlie went to his locker.

"No!" he gasped when he saw it open. The contents of it—his clothes, toiletries and Christmas gifts—scattered on the floor. "What's going on?"

Moments later, Gus returned.

"Master MacCready?" Brother Simon gasped, his voice sounding concerned. He looked at the mess on the floor.

"There's more, Brother Simon," Charlie said, and took him over to his cubicle.

"Where's your key?" he whispered in Charlie's ear.

Charlie pat his chest. "Right here."

"Oh, thank heaven. Do you have any idea who would have done this?"

"Just one," Charlie answered. "Kenneth DeVries."

"Really?" Brother Simon said pulling his head back and giving Charlie a curious look. "Why him?"

"I think he's mad at me."

"Again, I ask, why?"

"He's been after me for months wanting to buy my Saint Christopher medal."

"You didn't!"

"No," Charlie shook his head. "There's no way I would part with it. But Howard and I thought, since Kenneth was willing to pay whatever I asked for it, we could buy another one in town and sell that one to him."

"You didn't!"

"Yes, we did. Today after lunch we followed him. He met with a man out in the garage parking lot. From what we could tell, he wasn't fooled by the medal and slapped Kenneth. I think Kenneth's mad at me."

"Well, it would seem. Leave this and come with me."

Charlie followed his prefect. He was not sure if he was in trouble, or if Brother Simon was mad at him. Since Brother Simon always looked angry, it was hard to tell. They walked down the stairs to the first floor. Charlie realized they were headed for Abbot Ambrose's office.

"Sit here," Brother Simon instructed, pointing at the chair against the wall next to the Abbot's door. He knocked lightly on the door, then entered the office, closing the door behind him.

Charlie craned his neck and turned his ear toward the door in an attempt to hear what was going on inside.

"So, eavesdropping again?"

Charlie jumped and looked up at Brother Owen.

"No," he lied.

Brother Owen straightened his back and glared at him. "You are a troublemaker," he snarled and continued on his way.

Charlie watched the foyer door close behind the prefect. He looked up and down the hall to be sure no one else was around before turning his head to listen again. Just then the office door opened and Brother Simon looked out.

"Master MacCready, you may come in."

Charlie stood up nervously. He was not sure what to expect inside, but went anyway. Abbot Ambrose sat behind his desk. Father Mark was seated in the chair in front of it by the door.

"Please, have a seat," the Abbot offered, motioning toward the chairs behind Charlie.

Charlie turned around and gave a slight start. Seated in two of the three chairs were Howard and Kenneth. Charlie took the seat between them. He could feel Kenneth's icy stare but dared not look at him.

"Master MacCready," Abbot Ambrose began. "I understand that your cubicle and locker have been ransacked and that you suspect Master DeVries?"

Charlie nervously glanced out of the corner of his eyes at Kenneth. Kenneth was still staring at him.

"Yes, Father," Charlie answered.

"Why is that?"

Charlie looked at Howard. Howard frowned and looked at the floor. It was obvious to Charlie that he was on his own. Slowly he explained about the medal and what Howard and he had witnessed. When he was finished, he sat quietly bracing himself for what he knew would be a stern response.

"Master Miller, is this true?" the Abbot asked.

"Yes, Father Abbot."

"I see. And Master DeVries, did you ransack Master MacCready's locker and cubicle?"

Charlie looked at Kenneth. Kenneth had his head down but was still glaring at him. Charlie did not look away. He wanted to hear the answer.

"I want what I paid for," he said.

"Father Abbot, if I may," Brother Simon spoke up.

Abbot Ambrose nodded.

"Master DeVries, as I understood Master MacCready, you asked to buy his Saint Christopher medal. Is that correct?"

"Yes."

"Master MacCready, whose money bought the medal you sold to Master DeVries?"

"Mine."

"So, the medal was, in fact, your Saint Christopher."

"Yes."

"Master DeVries, did you not tell Master MacCready to 'name his price'?"

"Yes," he answered through clenched teeth.

"Did you receive the medal?"

"Not the one I thought I was getting. I wanted the other one."

"Why's that?"

Kenneth looked at the floor for a moment, apparently thinking about his answer. "Because I wanted it."

"And you always get what you want," Brother Simon added.

"I've heard enough," Abbot Ambrose said. "Master DeVries, while I do not agree with what these two have done, you bear the fault. Let this serve as a lesson for you. You will report to Brother Simon this Saturday for two hours of work crew.

"Master MacCready, I will leave you to clean up your locker and cubicle. Master Miller, you will assist him."

"Yes, Father," Howard answered for them.

"You two boys are excused. I would still like to speak with Master DeVries."

Charlie and Howard quickly left the office and headed for their dorm.

"I thought we were done for," Howard confessed.

"So did I," Charlie agreed. "What happened? And what about the fire alarm?"

"When I went to put away my binoculars, I ran into DeVries coming out of our dorm. His face was red and sweaty. When I saw what he did, I chased after him. Only Father Mark caught us both running in the hall and called us to the office. That's when the fire alarm went off."

"Who pulled it?"

"I don't know."
"Was there a fire?"
"I don't know that either," Howard answered.

ACCUSATIONS

The smell of burnt vinyl still lingered in the air inside the Abbey Church. Charlie and Howard stood in front of the place where the large nativity set was displayed.

"I can't believe someone would actually set fire to a manger scene, inside a church no less," Howard whispered. "Wouldn't you think you'd be afraid lightning would strike you dead on the spot?"

"Yeah," Charlie acknowledged. "Rick is never going to believe this. Does anyone know what caused it?"

"Someone lit a candle and set it on the floor in back. When the candle burnt down, it lit the straw and poof!"

"Returning to the scene of your crime?" Brother Owen said, looking down his nose at the two of them.

Howard and Charlie jumped, and turned around just in time to see Brother Owen disappear into the sanctuary.

"What is his problem?" Charlie asked, and shook his head.

"Ignore him. He's still angry about last year when Larry's father hit Dale."

"I know. I had nothing to do with it, so why is he mad at me?"

"I don't know. Forget it." Howard turned back to the charred floor. "So, who do you think is setting these fires?"

"I can't prove it but I think it's DeVries."

"Why him?"

"I don't know; he just gives me the creeps. It's just a feeling I have inside."

"Just because he's after your medal?"

"No. I don't think it's related to that."

"Well, I wish the police would find whoever it is and quit looking at me," Howard sighed. "I'm tired of being questioned."

"What time do you have?" Charlie asked.

"It's nearly lights out. We better head back to the dorm."

The two left the church and headed up the stairs.

"Too bad your pocket watch doesn't work," Howard said.

"Yeah," Charlie agreed and pulled it from the pocket of his cassock.

"Don't you think it's a strange gift? I mean, giving someone a watch that doesn't work?"

"I don't know. It was my grandfather's. Maybe she thought I'd like it for sentimental reasons." He put the watch to his ear and shook it. It rattled slightly. "Yep, it's broken." He stuck the watch back into his pocket. "Think Rick's back from Christmas break yet?"

"Probably. I'm really not in the mood to listen to how wonderful his Christmas was."

"Agreed."

When the boys entered their dorm, the lights were already dimmed, which meant no loud talking. Charlie glanced in the direction of Rick's cubicle and saw it was still dark. *Perhaps he's already in bed,* he thought to himself. He quickly changed into his pajamas and took his pocket watch from the pocket of his cassock.

He crawled beneath his covers and pulled his writing tablet out of his nightstand drawer. He settled back and began another letter to his grandmother. Perhaps, if he asked her again about the watch, she would tell him why she sent it.

He just sealed the envelope when Brother Simon walked up.

"Time for lights out, boys. Good night."

"Good night, Brother Simon," Howard answered. He put his comic book on his nightstand and turned off his lamp.

Charlie sat up in his bed for a moment longer. He looked out the window at the snow-covered Great Lawn. He imagined headlights were moving up the road toward the hilltop. His parents had finally returned for him. He imagined seeing the car pull around the side road, driving right up to the portico below. Then it stopped. The car door opened and Rick stepped out. Charlie shook his head. He was not imagining it. It was Rick. Why was he so late? Charlie lay down and waited for the sound of Rick returning to his cubicle.

"Charlie? Charlie?"

Charlie opened his eyes and looked around. It was still dark. He glanced at the clock on Howard's nightstand. It was two in the morning. He must have fallen asleep waiting for Rick.

"Charlie, get your robe on and come to my office," Brother Simon said.

Suddenly a wave of panic rushed over Charlie. He thought about his grandmother. Has something happened to her? He thought about his parents, had they come for him? He quickly slipped his robe on and made his way out of the dorm.

Once in the hallway he spotted Kenneth walking back to his dorm and the mystery was gone. He knocked on the office door.

"Please, come in, Master MacCready," Father Mark invited. "Have a seat."

Charlie sat down in the chair next to Brother Owen. He looked at them.

"We woke you up because someone has shredded Master DeVries bed sheets," Father Mark explained.

"And he thinks I did it?"

Father Mark looked at Brother Simon, then back at Charlie. "Yes," he answered.

"Why would I do that? It doesn't make sense."

"He thinks it's retaliation for his earlier transgression."

"You mean when he trashed my locker and cubicle," Charlie said bluntly feeling more annoyed by the second. "I didn't do it. I don't even step foot into Saint Peter. For that matter, no one I know who isn't a member of that dorm goes in there."

"Is that so?" Father Mark challenged.

"As far as I know," Charlie said with conviction. "If you ask me, I say he did it himself."

"Using your same logic," Father Mark said rocking back in his chair. "Why would he do that?"

"To draw suspicion away from himself. To make him the victim, then everyone would be looking the other way," Charlie explained. "And if you want to know, I think he's the one behind the fires, too."

Father Mark looked at Brother Simon again. Charlie could not tell if he believed him or was getting upset with his frankness. Either way, Charlie just wanted to go back to bed and forget this whole thing. He was tired of talking about Kenneth.

"Well, you certainly do have some strong opinions," Father Mark finally spoke. "I suggest you keep this quiet."

"So you believe me?"

"I didn't say that," Father Mark snapped. "Just that we don't need to start spreading rumors. If I hear of this from anyone, there will be consequences. Now go on back to bed."

"Okay." Charlie nodded. "Good night."

The sun seemed to rise early the next morning. Since returning to bed, Charlie scarcely slept a wink. He could not stop thinking about Kenneth's accusation that he had ripped up his sheets. He wanted desperately to tell Howard, but remembered Father Mark's threat.

Breakfast was a welcome diversion. Rick was back and seemed a bit preoccupied. Even Gus noticed, but did not let it stop him from eating his oatmeal.

"So, you got in late last night," Charlie said.

Rick looked across the table. "Yeah, snow."

Charlie and Howard exchanged glances.

"Okay, Walters, what's up? Didn't get that little something you were hoping for this Christmas?" Howard asked.

Rick looked at Howard and glared. "None of your business."

"Rick, what's wrong?" Charlie asked in a gentle tone.

Rick sat back in his chair and pushed his bowl away. "If you must know, my parents are getting a divorce."

"That was sudden. What happened?" Howard leaned forward and asked.

"It's been coming for some time. My mom and dad fought a lot over summer. I just found out that my dad moved out and got his own apartment. My sister and I spent Christmas, if you could call it that, with him."

"Rick, I'm so sorry."

Rick looked at Charlie. "Thanks. But the worst part is this might be my last year here."

"No!" Gus spoke up. "You can't leave me too."

Again, Howard and Charlie exchanged looks, the concern evident in both their faces.

"I didn't say it *was*, Gus. I said *might*. I won't know until my parents go to court."

"Isn't there something or someone that can help? I mean, you're here because you want to be a priest, right?" Howard said.

"Yeah," Rick nodded. "My mom is looking into getting some financial aid from the Diocese just in case my dad won't pay anymore."

"So, there's hope you can stay. See, Gus, there's nothing to worry about," Charlie said earnestly.

"Well, this was certainly turned out to be a Christmas break to remember," Howard said.

"So, what happened around here?" Rick asked.

The boys met in the bell tower after breakfast and Howard filled Rick in on the medal, the fire and Charlie's ransacked bed.

"So, who do you think is setting the fires?" Rick asked.

"I don't know," Charlie answered shrugging his shoulders.

"What?" Howard scoffed. "I thought you said yesterday you thought DeVries was behind it."

Charlie cringed and looked panicked. "I changed my mind."

Howard eyed him. "What's going on, MacCready."

"Nothing."

"You're lying!" Rick snapped back.

Again, Charlie looked around. "Okay," he whispered. "But if word gets out that I said anything, I'm gonna be in trouble." He then explained to the three of them what happened during the night.

"I will be in so much trouble if any of this gets out. So you

have to promise me, you won't say a word to anyone."
 They all agreed.

DEVRIES

The warmth of the winter sun was a pleasant change from the cold snows. Charlie and Father Cecil slowly walked along the road to the west of the Great Lawn. While its lush green grass looked inviting, the ground was too soft to walk on without ruining their shoes, as Father Cecil told him. Charlie did not mind.

"So, how have your classes been?" Father Cecil asked.

"Actually, not as hard as I imagined. Except Geometry. I hate that class. It makes no sense. I don't understand theorems and hypothesis. Give me Algebra any day. I can do that."

Father Cecil chuckled quietly. "It'll all work out. What about your other classes?"

"Biology is okay. I almost threw up in class, though, when we had to dissect a frog. Thank goodness Howard did most of the cutting stuff. Rumor has it in spring we're going to have to catch bugs."

"Yeah, I heard that Father Boniface was still adding to his bug collection. Some of God's creations are a bit creepy indeed. So, what's your favorite class?"

"That's a tough one." Charlie squinted while he thought. Just then he spotted the dark car parked along the side of the road. He stopped.

"What is it?" Father Cecil asked.

"It's the same black car that I saw on Christmas. Remember I told you about Kenneth and the driver?"

"Do you see anyone?"

"No."

"Well, be careful and let us proceed, quietly."

The two continued on their walk. As they neared the car Charlie saw that it was empty. Father Cecil tightened his grip and cocked his head as he listened. Then Charlie heard them too, two distinct voices coming from the woods beside the road. The deeper voice, obviously the driver, sounded angry.

"I've been reading in the newspaper what has been happening up here. It had better stop! Am I making myself clear?"

"It's not me this time."

"And that's what you said at your previous school and the one before that. If it doesn't stop you will be locked up. Is that what you want?"

"No."

"Then make it stop. Now, about our other matter."

"Dad, I've tried but he's got it on a chain around his neck and never takes it off."

"It's not good enough! I need that medal. Wait! Someone's coming."

Charlie jumped and the two resumed walking.

"Did you hear that?" Charlie asked, his heart pounding in his chest.

"Yes, I heard it."

"We've got to tell someone."

"Stay calm, Charlie," Father Cecil said, patting Charlie's arm while he held onto him. "Perhaps we should head back to the Abbey. Just up the road here is a fork that will lead us back by the barns and pool."

"Okay," Charlie agreed.

The two walked in silence until they reached the Abbey.

"Let me talk with Abbot Ambrose about what we heard," Father Cecil said. "You go catch up with your friends, and stay away from that Kenneth boy."

"Okay."

Charlie left Father Cecil outside the Abbot's door. He raced up the stairs and the dorm. Howard was not in their cubicle. He hurried off to the tower. Just when he reached the doors of Saint Peter dorm they opened. Dougary, Travis and Kenneth walked into the hall.

"Not so fast, MacCreepy." Dougary threw back his head and said. He stepped in front of Charlie while Travis and Kenneth circled around back.

"Out of my way, I'm busy." Charlie started to walk around Dougary but Dougary stepped in front of him. He put his hand on Charlie's chest and gave him a slight shove back.

"What's the hurry? We just want to talk to you."

"About what?"

"You have something that doesn't belong to you," Kenneth said, stepping in front of Charlie.

"Like what?"

"That medal. I paid you twenty bucks for it and I want it."

"You got the medal you paid for, remember?"

"That wasn't it. I wanted the medal that is on the chain around your neck."

Charlie's hand instantly felt the key, locket and metal beneath his robes. "No way."

"I think you should rethink your answer," Kenneth snarled and stepped forward.

Charlie stepped back, bumping into Travis.

"Hey!" Travis yelled and shoved Charlie forward into Kenneth.

"You guys are all crazy! Get out of my way!" Charlie shouted. He started around Kenneth but Kenneth grabbed him and threw him to the floor.

"I want that medal!" he shouted, and lunged at Charlie. His knees pinned Charlie's arms to the floor while his hands ripped at Charlie's surplice and cassock.

"Get off me!" Charlie shouted.

"Master DeVries, what is going on?" Brother Conrad shouted.

Kenneth ignored the prefect. Dougary and Travis slipped away.

"Get off of him!" Brother Conrad yelled, grabbing Kenneth's arm and pulling him off Charlie.

Kenneth struggled with the thin monk, who was surprisingly stronger than he looked.

"That is enough!" Brother Conrad said, and slapped Kenneth across the face.

Kenneth instantly stood still, stunned. His cheek turned red and Charlie could see the print of Brother Conrad's hand.

"Now, what is this about?"

"He was trying to steal my medal," Charlie answered, and climbed to his feet. He straightened his robes and looked at the torn collar of his surplice.

"It's my medal. I paid for it!" Kenneth snapped back.

"Oh, I heard about this," Brother Conrad said. "Master DeVries, let's see what Father Mark has to say about this? Master MacCready, give your surplice to the brothers in the laundry, they'll make sure it gets mended."

"Yes, Brother Conrad."

Charlie waited until Brother Conrad and Kenneth were out of sight before he crawled into the bell tower. When he reached the top, Howard was looking out the north arch. He turned around and his mouth dropped open in surprise.

"What happened to you?"

"DeVries. This time he attacked me and tried to rip the medal from my neck. Brother Conrad stopped him, and is taking him to see Father Mark."

"Are you serious?

"Yes. But there is something more," Charlie said and glanced out the north arch. He looked across the Great Lawn to where he saw the black car, but it was gone. He told Howard everything he and Father Cecil heard. "Why would someone lie about something like that?"

"I don't know," Howard said and shook his head. "This is getting weird."

"I left Father Cecil with Abbot Ambrose when we came back. He's going to tell him."

"I don't know what to say. This is strange. The only thing in the newspaper has been about the fires. Are you sure his father said Kenneth was doing it?"

"He didn't say it outright but I'm sure of it. My suspicions about him are right."

"I think it's good that Father Cecil heard it too. Maybe they'll listen too with it coming from an adult."

"I hope so. But how does Kenneth's father know about my medal and why does he want it?"

"I don't know. Are you sure you don't know him?"

"I'm sure."

"Maybe he knows your grandmother. You can ask her.

Have you tried to call her lately?"

"Not since the time my uncle answered."

"Maybe we should try again. I'll get her on the line, then hand you the phone."

The two left the belfry and slipped down the stairs to the first floor. A small closet between the seminarians' refectory and theirs was converted into a public telephone booth. Charlie gave Howard the number and waited while he dialed. After making sure Charlie's grandmother was able to talk, he handed the receiver to Charlie.

"Hi Grandma."

"Hello, Charlie. What a pleasant surprise. Howard sounds like such a nice boy. How are you doing?"

"I'm doing okay. I have a question though. Remember I told you about that new kid, Kenneth?"

"Yes."

"Well, he's been after the medal you gave me."

"He hasn't taken it has he?" Her voice sounded panicked.

"No, Grandma. But I found out today he isn't an orphan and that his father is the one who wants the medal. Grandma, do you know anyone by the last name DeVries?

"Grandma, are you still there?"

"Yes, Charlie. I'm here," she answered, her voice faint and strained. "Charlie you mustn't let that medal out of your sight. Whatever you do, don't give it to him."

"Why? What's so important about it?"

"I can't tell you right now. Not yet. But soon. I promise."

"Do you know him, Grandma?"

"Yes, Charlie. I know him. He was an acquaintance of your father's, and not a nice man. Stay away from him."

"I will."

"Charlie, I have to go. Someone's here."

"Who are you talking to?" Charlie recognized his uncle's voice in the background. He quickly hung the receiver back on its hook and sat back against the wall, staring at the phone.

"So, what did she say? Does she know him?" Howard asked.

Charlie looked at Howard. "Yes, he knew my father."

"What?" Howard raised his voice.

"She said to stay away from him. He's not a nice man."

"Duh! We already know that. Come on. Let's go back to the dorm. DeVries won't bother us there."

THE TOWER

Charlie glanced at the line of boys from Saint Peter dorm while he stood behind Howard waiting for the refectory doors to open. He could not help noticing Kenneth staring at him in his usual manner: head tilted down and eyes looking up, jaws tight, brow furrowed. Charlie looked away.

Once inside the refectory and seated, the waiters began to serve dinner. Charlie took a deep breath and smiled.

"Beef stew," he announced to Howard and Gus. "Fresh hot dinner rolls and butter."

"Come on, you can't smell butter," Gus groaned.

"Did I say butter?" Charlie asked.

"You talked to Sister Anthony, didn't you?" Howard laughed. "What a phony!"

Charlie laughed with his friends.

"Watch your back, Charlie. DeVries is after you," Ted Wilson whispered into Charlie's ear as he passed behind him.

Charlie jumped and turned around but Ted was already halfway back to the kitchen.

"What's that about?" Howard asked.

"Don't know," Charlie answered. He glanced at Kenneth, who was still glaring at him. Charlie rolled his eyes and shook his head before looking away.

After dinner, Charlie, Howard, Rick and Gus gathered in the bell tower. The evening air had just the right amount of crispness to feel refreshing but not too cold. Charlie took a deep breath and looked out toward the south. The setting sun cast long shadows across the butte. His thoughts turned to the medal.

"What do you think DeVries will do next?" Rick asked.

"Who cares?" Howard answered.

"Charlie should," Gus spoke up. "He's got Travis in his pocket, not to mention Dougary."

"Well, I seriously doubt he'll try anything again," Howard said confidently.

"I don't know about that," Gus shook his head. "Ted seems to think he will."

"What do we care what Wilson thinks, he's a traitor for moving into Saint Peter dorm in the first place."

"No," Charlie turned around. "Father Abbott asked him to move."

"And you know this how?" Rick asked.

"Because he told me. He said Father Abbot needed someone who could watch out for the younger boys. He doesn't want another Dougary."

Rick opened his mouth to say something but then closed it.

"I still don't think DeVries will try anything more," Howard insisted.

The winds changed direction. Suddenly the scent of smoke wafted up, filling the belfry. The boys choked and covered their mouths and noses. They looked around, searching for the source of the smoke. Slowly they crept to the hole in the floor beneath the bells and looked down. Through the smoke they could see the flickering of flames on the ground below. Just then the fire siren began to blow.

"Quick! Let's get out of here!" Howard yelled through his sleeve.

The rickety wooden stairs shook violently under the weight of the boys. They stopped and held fast to the handrails.

"What's—" Gus gasped just as bolts holding the stairs to the brick wall pulled loose. The staircase lurched.

"Run!" Howard yelled but it was too late. The staircase tilted and fell away from the wall sending the boys screaming and crashing to the floor.

Amid groans and coughs and the blaring siren, the dazed boys crawled to the door. Once safely on the fourth floor with the door closed behind them, they took in deep breaths of fresh air.

"Come on!" Charlie said and started down the stairs. The others quickly followed.

Outside, the fire trucks had arrived, along with three police cars. While the firemen extinguished the fire in the base of the tower the police, Abbott Ambrose, Father Mark and Father Vicar were huddled together away from everyone else. Charlie and the other three joined the other members of their dorm on the Great Lawn.

"Where have you guys been?" Ted Wilson asked.

"Why aren't you with your dorm?" Howard snapped at him.

Ted ignored Howard and turned toward Charlie. "Did you hear they caught the kid who's been setting the fires?"

"They did?" Charlie said not hiding his surprise.

"Yeah, we don't know who it is yet, but I bet he gets expelled."

"Ya think?" Howard said sarcastically.

Ted again ignored him, and continued craning his neck to see if he could catch a glimpse of the culprit.

"I need to sit down," Charlie said and walked over to the bench by the nearest pond. Howard, Gus and Rick followed.

"Do you think the guy did it on purpose?" Gus asked.

"I don't think he lit the fire by accident," Howard answered.

"No. I mean do you think he knew we were up there?"

Charlie looked at Gus, then across the way at the flashing lights of the police cars. Before he could say a word, Howard spoke.

"No one but us knows about the tower; that is except Father Mark and Abbot Ambrose."

"I wouldn't be too sure about that," Rick spoke up. "Remember Dale also knows about it. And I've seen you guys up there several times when I was walking around the grounds. It's not all that secret."

Howard glared at Rick.

"I doubt he knew," Charlie said putting an end to their arguing before it became heated. "I think it was just a coincidence."

"Look!" Gus said pointing at the policemen.

Charlie stood up to get a better view. The group of police moved toward one of the cars. One opened the back door and someone climbed inside. It seemed that the officers were intentionally blocking their view.

"Did you see who it was?" he asked.

"No," they all answered.

Charlie noticed Father Mark had something draped over his arm and he realized it was the cassock and surplice of the boy in the back of the police car. In the red and blue flashing lights, Charlie could not make out the true color of the surplice.

Brother Simon walked over to the boys. "We are gathering in the auditorium. Come along." He ushered them toward the seminary building.

The auditorium was noisy. Charlie found four seats and quickly claimed them for his friends.

"Think they're going to tell us what is going on?" Gus asked.

"Don't know. Maybe they wanted us out of the way so they could take the pyro away in secret," Howard answered.

Charlie was not paying attention to them. He was searching the crowd, trying to figure out who was missing. He leaned closer to Howard.

"Dougary, Travis, Austin and Kenneth aren't here," he informed him.

Howard looked around. "Are you sure?"

"Yes," Charlie nodded.

"Well, this narrows it down some. It must be at least one of them."

"That's what I'm thinking," Charlie said and sat back up in his chair.

"Wonder how long we're gonna have to wait here," Rick complained.

The auditorium was built to keep the noise of the outside from coming in. As a result, even if the other boys were all silent, Charlie still would not be able to hear what was going on outside. He pulled his pocket watch from the pocket of his cassock and opened it.

"Still not working?" Howard asked.

"Nah," Charlie answered and shook his head.

"I said it before and I'll say it again, why would someone give someone a broken watch for a present?"

"It was my grandfather's," Charlie said, in his

grandmother's defense. "Maybe she didn't know it was broken?"

"Well, we've been in here for an hour in case that is what you wanted to know," Howard said.

"Thanks." Charlie looked at the engraving on the inside of the face cover. He silently read the inscription. "The Dark Angel."

The doors in the back of the auditorium opened and the room fell silent. Everyone turned to see who had entered.

Abbot Ambrose walked up the aisle to the stage, followed closely by all of the prefects and Father Mark. Abbot Ambrose stood in the center of the stage with his hands hidden beneath his robes. He looked at the boys and waited until the prefects were standing shoulder to shoulder behind him.

"Good evening. I want you all to pay very close attention to what I'm about to say. I will not repeat it and I will not answer any questions. We will speak of this no more," Abbot Ambrose began.

"For the past nine months our home has been in an upheaval as you are quite well aware. Tonight, peace has finally been restored. The person responsible for setting the fires has been caught along with his accomplices."

Charlie looked at Howard with a confused expression.

"Master Kenneth DeVries is in police custody and has been removed from the hilltop. Today we finally received his records. As it turns out, he has been here under false pretense. His parents are very much alive and they went to great lengths to conceal from us Master DeVries's history of setting fires. Had we known about this, he would never have been permitted on the property."

"Who are his accomplices?" Charlie whispered to Howard. Howard shrugged. Charlie looked toward the back of the auditorium and noticed Dougary, Travis and Austin standing near the door. He turned back around.

"Master DeVries and his parents are facing arson charges. I am confident that justice will prevail.

"Now, as of this moment, his name shall never be uttered on this hilltop again. Is this clear?"

Abbot Ambrose looked at the boys as each nodded his understanding and agreement.

"Very well," he continued. "The fire this evening was confined to the bell tower." He looked at Howard and Charlie. "There was only minor damage done but no permanent structural harm. I ask that you all stay clear of the area until repairs are made."

Howard nodded silently.

"You may all return to your dorms. Remember, it is past nine o'clock so silence is to be observed. Lights out will be in one hour. You may all be dismissed."

Before anyone moved, Abbot Ambrose and the prefects left the auditorium. Howard leaned closer to Charlie while the four of them walked through the door.

"I can't believe it. You told them he was the pyro."

"He also said Gus was," Rick reminded them.

Howard glared at him. "Whatever."

"I don't care. It's finally over," Charlie said. "Maybe now we can sleep without having to keep one eye open at night."

THE MUSEUM

The dull roar of the lawn mower echoed across the hilltop. The scent of freshly cut grass was thick, masking the aroma of the spring flowers and blossoming cherry trees. Charlie looked out at Black Butte from the south arch of the bell tower. It had taken the brothers two months to repair the damage caused by the fire and the staircase.

Charlie pulled the chain around his neck until his treasures popped from beneath his robes. He turned the medal over and squinted while he tried to read the engraving.

"I wish I knew what is so special about this medal that Mr. DeVries would want it so badly," he said.

Howard turned around from the north arch. "I wish your grandmother would spill it. I mean, tell you. What's the big mystery?"

"I know," Charlie lamented. "What time is it?"

"It's one o'clock. Why?"

"I'm going to help Father Ignatius in the museum. He's just about finished setting it up."

"I'll pass." Howard shook his head and turned back to the

view.

"See ya around." Charlie made his way down the new staircase. The wooden steps and handrail felt more secure than the old one and made Charlie feel safer.

Moments later he was in the basement of the monastery wing. The basement hall was dark except for the light from the doorway at the far end. Charlie was used to it and no longer afraid.

"Hi, Father Ignatius," he greeted as he walked into the museum.

The small monk turned around from hanging a framed photograph, and smiled. "You're just in time. Give me a hand with this, will you?"

"Sure."

Charlie took the large frame from Father Ignatius and held it.

"Looks like you're almost finished," he said looking around the room.

"It does look that way, but there is still a lot to do before we'll be ready to open." He pounded the nail and hook into the wall. "There, that should do it." He put the hammer down and took the picture from Charlie. With a couple failed attempts to hook the wire on the back, he finally succeeded and stepped back. "What do you think?"

Charlie looked at the picture, and remembered Father Ignatius had not finished telling him about Black Butte.

"That's first Abbey building?" he asked.

"Ah, good eye, Master McCready," Father Ignatius commended him. "This is. If you look closely, you will see the first Abbot standing to the right of the front door." He pointed at the black-and-white picture.

"What happened to it?"

"I'm afraid it burned to the ground," answered Father Ignatius.

"Is that why they call it Black Butte?"

"Oh, no. According to the records, when the first monks arrived here from the abbey in Germany in 1882 to establish an abbey, they bought the mountain and several surrounding farms from the townspeople. In 1883, the brothers completed building this version of the abbey at the base of the mountain. However, not all of the farmers were happy about it. Some felt the brothers had taken advantage of the superstitious and fearful townspeople buying up the land for less than it was worth.

"At first, they tried to scare our brothers away by hiding out in the forest and making chanting noises like the natives. That didn't work. Our brothers were not superstitious. When they didn't leave, the farmers became angry. Fueled by that anger and a few pints from the local saloon, they set fire to the building in the middle of the night. Luckily, everyone was able to get out safely, but the entire structure was lost."

"Wow!" Charlie gasped. "Did they catch the people who did it?"

"No." Father Ignatius shook his head. "But as it happened, when the faithful of the town found out about the fire, they opened their homes and their purses. In no time the brothers set to work on a new Abbey building."

"On Black Butte," Charlie interrupted.

"Yes, that's right. Only, it still wasn't called Black Butte at that time." Father Ignatius nodded. "Work began in the spring of 1896 and by the winter of that year, the brothers moved back into their own home." Father Ignatius pointed to the framed picture hanging beside the first.

Charlie nodded. He had seen that old photograph before. The second Abbey building resembled a square castle with its tall, three-story walls dotted by small windows. It had a bell tower that rose out of the center courtyard high above the rooftop.

"Sadly, just fourteen short years later the Abbey suffered another fire. I was a novice at the time. I'll never forget that night." He paused while he looked at the picture. His hands began to tremble. He slipped them beneath his robes.

"This time it was not at the hands of the farmers," he began slowly, quietly, in a near whisper, his eyes locked in a stare at the image of the old Abbey. "It was in the summer of 1910. There was a horrible thunderstorm that night. The winds were blowing extra hard. I was awakened by the loudest roll of thunder I've ever heard. It shook the building. I looked out through my cell window. The sky all around the hilltop was lit up with one flash of lightning after another. I was terrified but I couldn't pull myself away from the sight.

"I'm not sure how long I was standing there before I noticed the flames. They started outside the chapel and quickly moved up the outside wall. I ran to the hallway, and began knocking on doors, waking everyone up. I was yelling fire. Once everyone was safely outside, we tried to put the fire out, but the winds were too strong and the flames too hot. Even the rain didn't stop it. By morning it was over. Somehow, by the Grace of God, the bell tower survived. See," he pointed toward another photo.

Charlie stepped forward and looked at the picture. The bell tower stood in the center of the charred remains of the Abbey. Its stone walls were crumbled and blackened by soot and ash.

"What did you do then?"

"We rebuilt, this time on the north hilltop. We cleared the ground and put in a water tower in case there was ever another disastrous fire. The new Abbey was built in stages: first the monastery wing, then Abbey Church. The student wing wasn't completed until later." Again, he pointed at another black-and-white photograph.

Charlie smiled, recognizing the familiar building.

"The bells in the tower are the same bells that survived the second fire. That's why when that boy started the fire in the base of the tower, the entire Abbey was upset. I'm thankful to the fire department and the bravery of the brothers for putting it out quickly."

"Me too," Charlie nodded. He looked at the glass display case beneath the pictures. It was filled with an old book, a blackened crucifix and other artifacts. "What are these?"

"These are some of the things that were found after the second fire. They were in the catacombs beneath the Abbey."

"Were people buried in the catacombs?"

"The founding Abbot and a couple of the older monks who came here with him were buried there, but they were moved to the Abbey's cemetery years ago."

"Are the catacombs still there?"

Father Ignatius appeared distracted by his thoughts while he looked at the shelves of artifacts. "I think so," he answered. "What do you say you grab the dust mop and give the floor a final going over? Tomorrow's our big opening day, right after the graduation ceremony. We want the place looking its best."

"Sure," Charlie said, and went to get the mop.

After he finished cleaning the museum, Charlie headed up to Father Cecil's room. He could not stop thinking about the second Abbey building and the catacombs.

"Good to see you, Charlie," Father Cecil greeted when he opened the door.

Charlie still was not used to Father Cecil's sense of humor. He frowned not knowing how to answer.

"Come in. Come in. Have a seat. So, how has your day been?"

Charlie waited until Father Cecil was seated in his chair in the corner before he sat down at the table.

"I finished helping Father Ignatius with the museum. It's all ready for the opening tomorrow afternoon."

"Good. Can't wait to see it."

Again, Charlie frowned. "I have a question maybe you can answer," Charlie said.

"I'll try. What is it?"

"Father Ignatius told me all about the history of the Abbey. About the two fires that destroyed the first and second Abbey buildings...."

"Yes?"

"How did Black Butte come to be called, 'Black Butte'?"

Father Cecil smiled. "Well, the obvious reason would be due to the fire that burned the second Abbey. However, some may argue it was a name given it by the townsfolk because of the color of our habits."

Charlie nodded to himself. "Both reasons make sense, I guess. What about the catacombs?"

The color drained from Father Cecil's face. He turned his head toward Charlie, seemingly staring at the wall behind him. "Who told you about those?"

"Father Ignatius," Charlie answered hesitantly.

"He should never have said anything!"

"Why? What's the harm?"

"They're dangerous. A curious boy could get himself seriously hurt if he were to go out there. Over the years the catacombs have fallen into disrepair and parts of them have even caved in. It's just not safe. Father Ignatius should've known better."

"It's okay, Father. I won't say anything."

"I know you won't. But you have to promise me that you will stay away from there. I mean it. It's very serious."

Charlie hesitated for a moment, then agreed.

THE RUINS

Charlie stood in the bell tower, staring out the south archway at Black Butte. He had slipped away from the graduation party and the grand opening of the museum to be alone with his thoughts. Unconsciously, he fumbled with the Saint Christopher medal that hung on the chain around his neck.

The sound of laughter distracted him. He left the south arch and walked around the bells to the north side. He looked down at the crowd gathered on the Great Lawn. Someone was taking a picture of one of the graduating boys. Charlie figured it was one of the student boys since it appeared to be family around him. Resident boys usually did not have that much fanfare.

Charlie turned around as though being pulled back to the south view. He took a step and stopped.

"I know I promised," he said out loud. "But I have to see what's out there."

Cautiously, Charlie slipped out the back door and headed down the path past Our Lady of the Subway and the cemetery. In no time he reached the overgrown dirt and gravel road that led off toward Black Butte. A rusted chain blocked the entrance to the road. Charlie looked around to be sure no one was watching him.

Confident he was alone, he slipped around the end post and headed down the road. He stayed near the trees, just in case someone happened to look in his direction. They would not see him. With every step he took, he began to feel his anxiety ebb.

I did it, he thought to himself. I can't believe how easy it was. I should have done it a long time ago. What's the harm anyway?

The road wound its way through the trees until it came to a dead end. The forest had reclaimed its land. Tall trees had obliterated any trace of the road. Thick ferns and undergrowth hid any evidence of gravel left behind. Still, Charlie pressed on. He knew by the slope of the land that the burned-out Abbey would be at the top of the rise.

In just a few minutes he emerged from the forest to a clearing. He stopped and stared in awe at the sight before him. The tower in the center of the old building still stood tall but its roof and belfry were deteriorated. All around it were piles of stone blocks still scarred from the fire.

Slowly Charlie crept closer. He glanced over his shoulder in the direction of the Abbey, at the bell tower, and wondered if Howard could see him. Charlie could not see the tower and felt sure Howard could not see him even with his binoculars. He relaxed a bit more and continued on his way.

Howard was right. There really was not much to see. Just a bunch of rocks piled on top of each other. The bell tower was neat though. Charlie walked over to it and looked up. It did not look nearly as tall as his tower. Nor was it as wide. He stuck his head in the doorway and looked up. There was a pile of weathered wooden planks inside. Charlie assumed they were once part of a staircase much like the one that used to be in his tower. He turned away from the tower and walked around the overgrown courtyard. He tried to imagine the old building and where Father Ignatius's window would have been.

Carefully he made his way from the center to the outside of the ruins. While he walked around, looking at the stones that were once part of the building, he rubbed his thumb over the face of his medal.

Suddenly he stopped.

He tilted his head and stared at a large square block, at the worn engraving on its side. "1896," he said out loud. He turned the medal over and looked at the back.

"1896 NW 10 st," he read to himself. "A map." He looked around. "1896 northwest 10 steps. I wonder."

He walked over to the stone block and looked around. "Northwest," he repeated and turned to face that direction. He counted to himself as he took ten steps away from the block. Stopping, he looked around. He was standing in the clearing that surrounded the old Abbey. He looked at the ground and wondered if he was supposed to dig or if he was in the right place. He walked back to the stone and tried again, this time taking bigger steps. Still no clue. He tried it a few more times.

"Why couldn't this be easier," he said to himself while he looked at the ground.

"What was that?" a voice asked him.

Charlie turned around and saw a man sitting on the cornerstone. Immediately his heart began to pound against his chest. He recognized the man. It was Kenneth's father. Charlie took a step away.

"Nothing," he answered the man.

"So, you think you have discovered the meaning of the message on that medal?"

Charlie looked at the medal and quickly tucked it beneath

his robes. The man smiled. "How do you know about my medal?"

Mr. DeVries laughed. "Your father told me."

Charlie's eyes widened. "When? Where? Is he alive?"

He gave Charlie a confused look. "You're joking, right?"

"No."

Hopping down form the stone, he took a step toward Charlie. Charlie backed up.

"Your father told me about the medal a long time ago, before you were born, I'm guessing. Said he had the map to his family's fortune engraved on it."

Charlie put his hand over his heart, feeling the medal beneath his clothes.

"Why don't you be a good boy and hand it over?"

"No!" Charlie said sharply. He took another step back. His eyes still focused on Kenneth's father.

"I tried doing things the easy way, but that good-for-nothing son of mine couldn't control himself. So, now I guess it's time to do it myself. You have two choices, Chuckie. You can either hand it over to me, and not get hurt, or I can take it from you and all bets are off."

Charlie took another step and felt the ground move slightly beneath his feet. Kenneth's father stood up.

"Have it your way, kid." Mr. DeVries started toward Charlie. Charlie continued to back away feeling the ground tremble.

"Don't make this any harder than it has to be. Just hand over the medal you little brat!"

"No!" Charlie answered back defiantly. He turned and ran toward the woods as fast as he could.

"You bastard!" Mr. DeVries cursed and let out a frightened yell.

Charlie stopped and turned around when he reached the forest, but Mr. DeVries was gone. Slowly Charlie crept back into the clearing. He cocked his head and listened. Faint sounds of moaning seemed to come from the ground. Charlie spotted a hole in the ground that was not there before. Carefully he approached.

"Mr. DeVries?" he said into the hole.

There was no response, just pained groans.

Charlie looked around. "I'll go get help," he called down.

Without thinking of how he would explain being on Black Butte, Charlie quickly ran back to the Abbey. He located Howard by the food table on the Great Lawn, talking to Rick and Gus.

"Where have you been?" Howard asked.

Charlie tried to catch his breath before he spoke. "Black Butte," he answered. "Where's Brother Simon?"

"Are you nuts?" Howard snapped. "What were you doing out there?"

"You went to Black Butte?" Gus gasped in shock.

"Oh, now you've done it!" Rick shook his head.

"I need to find Brother Simon," Charlie repeated still panting.

Howard looked around at the crowd. "He's over there."

"Thanks. Come on." Charlie wove his way through the gathering until he reached his prefect. He stopped, and started to turn away when he saw that Brother Simon was talking with Father Mark and Abbot Ambrose, but bumped into Howard.

"Where're you going? I thought you wanted Brother Simon?"

"He's busy," Charlie said suddenly feeling nervous.

"Nonsense, here. Brother Simon, Charlie needs to talk to you," Howard called.

Brother Simon looked at Charlie and saw the sweat on his face. He excused himself, and left Father Mark and the Abbot standing together.

"Yes, Master MacCready?"

"Brother Simon, please don't get mad right away, I need your help. Well, actually, Mr. DeVries needs your help."

Brother Simon looked confused. "What are you talking about?"

"He went out to Black Butte," Howard blurted.

"You what?" Brother Simon shouted.

"I went out to Black Butte. I wanted to see it for myself. But Mr. DeVries showed up and he wanted my medal."

"You didn't give it to him, did you?" Brother Simon interrupted.

"No. But the ground gave way and I think Mr. DeVries is hurt."

Brother Simon thought for a moment. "Wait here." He went back to Father Mark and the Abbot and quickly filled them in. Abbot Ambrose grabbed a passing monk and gave him instructions.

Several minutes later, with the police and emergency medical workers help, Mr. DeVries was lifted out of the catacombs and placed on a stretcher. Charlie stood between Abbott Ambrose and Brother Simon and watched. Part of him felt sorry for Mr. DeVries. He did not like seeing anyone hurt, even if it was their own fault.

One of the officers walked over to them.

"Father Abbott," he acknowledged. "It appears that Mr. DeVries has a broken leg, but that is the least of his problems. He'll be facing charges of violation of his probation and trespassing, just to name a couple. I don't think you'll be hearing from him for a long time."

"That will be good." Abbot Ambrose nodded. While the policeman left, Abbot Ambrose turned toward Charlie. "I want to see you in my office in one hour. Don't be late."

Charlie hesitated while he stood in front of Abbot Ambrose's door. He wished that Howard, Rick or even Gus would have come with him. He supposed they wanted to keep their distance in case they would be in some sort of trouble too.

"Ave," came the response to his knock.

Slowly Charlie opened the door. Brother Simon looked up from his seat across the desk from Abbot Ambrose.

"Please, have a seat, son," Abbot Ambrose offered, holding out his hand toward the three chairs beside his desk.

Nervously Charlie sat in the middle one.

"What were you doing out there?"

"I don't know," Charlie answered. "I was looking out at the butte and it was as if something were drawing me to it. I had to go."

Brother Simon frowned. "Nonsense."

"Simon, please," Abbot Ambrose said then turned back to Charlie. "What did you expect to find?"

"I don't know." Charlie shrugged. He fumbled with the medal beneath his cassock. "I thought maybe there would be something out there that would help me figure out what is written on the back of the medal."

"And was there?"

"No." Charlie shook his head.

"So, how is it that Mr. DeVries was out there?"

"I don't know. I guess he followed me but I thought I was being careful."

"You're lucky you didn't fall into that hole," Brother Simon snapped.

"It wasn't there. I mean, it just appeared out of nowhere."

"I see," Abbot Ambrose said. "Evidently the ground and old timbers beneath couldn't support Mr. DeVries weight. Now do you see why we don't want you boys going out there?"

"Yes, Father Abbot." Charlie nodded. "I have a question."

Abbot Ambrose cocked his head and looked at Charlie.

"I thought Mr. DeVries was locked up?"

"No, Charlie. The courts fined him and gave him probation. Part of the agreement was that he would never step foot on our hilltop again. As for Master DeVries, he is in the state hospital psychiatric ward and will be there for a long time."

"I see." Charlie looked down at his chest as if seeing the medal beneath his cloths.

"Is there something else?" Abbot Ambrose asked, noticing Charlie's thoughtful expression.

"It's just that Mr. DeVries said my father told him that the engraving on the back of my medal was a map to my family's fortune."

"Interesting."

Charlie looked confused. "I don't understand. Do you know about the medal? Do you know where it is?"

"Charlie, you have to trust me when I tell you it's not time for you to know just yet."

"So you do know!"

"Yes, but to tell you now would not be wise. Please, be patient."

"It's not fair!" Charlie snapped. "Why give me the medal and then tell me to wait?"

"Charlie, your grandmother gave it to you because it was no longer safe for her to keep it. Please, trust me on this. When you are ready, I will tell you everything."

Charlie looked at his great-uncle and nodded.

"What about his punishment?" Brother Simon asked.

Abbot Ambrose studied Charlie for a moment. "What you are looking for is not out there," he said. "Promise me, you will never to go out there again?"

"Yes, Father Abbot, I promise." Charlie nodded.

"I have your solemn word on this?"

"Yes, cross my heart and hope to die."

Abbot Ambrose chuckled. "I don't think we need to go that far. At this time, we will forego any punishment. You are dismissed."

"Thank you, Father Abbot, Brother Simon. I won't let you down again."

"Let's hope not," Abbot Ambrose said.

ABOUT THE AUTHOR

James M. McCracken spent much of his teenage years away from his family in a seminary boarding school. It was there that his love of writing began. It is his experiences while at the boarding school that serve as the inspiration for the Charlie MacCready series.

James M. McCracken currently resides in Central Oregon. He is a longtime member of the writing group Becoming Fiction and the Northwest Independent Writers Association.

www.ingramcontent.com/pod-product-compliance
Lightning Source LLC
LaVergne TN
LVHW022002060526
838200LV00003B/61